"Don't look back! Run, you bastards! Run!"

Ardo ran next to Littlefield, the metal case banging wildly between them. His free hand held his rifle, swinging as it spewed carnage indiscriminately in his path. There was no effort to fire for effect—all he could do as he ran was random damage and add to the carnage already taking place.

The flames wrapped around Ardo as he crossed the line. The footing had already gotten difficult, the ground slick with charred and ruptured Zerg. Still the metal box banged against his leg, letting him know that Littlefield was still there, still running and pulling him forward.

An unearthly scream tore across the com channel. It continued, an ear-piercing squeal of terror. The internal temperature of his battle armor was growing by the moment. He could feel his hands and feet starting to blister. Suddenly he ran directly into a standing Zergling. Ardo screamed but did not stop, knocking the creature down in his rush before both vanished from each other amid the conflagration.

"Keep running, you dogs!" Breanne spat through the com channel. Her own voice had an edge to it Ardo had never heard before. Was she winded or just afraid? "Keep running and don't look back!"

Instinctively, Ardo looked.

STARCRAFT®

THE SPEED
OF DARKNESS

TRACY HICKMAN

POCKET BOOKS
New York   London   Toronto   Sydney

This book is a work of fiction. Names, characters, places and incidents are products of the author's imagination or are used fictitiously. Any resemblance to actual events or locales or persons, living or dead, is entirely coincidental.

An *Original* Publication of POCKET BOOKS

POCKET BOOKS, a division of Simon & Schuster, Inc.
1230 Avenue of the Americas, New York, NY 10020

ISBN: 0-671-04150-9

First Pocket Books printing June 2002

10 9 8 7 6 5 4 3

POCKET and colophon are registered trademarks of Simon & Schuster, Inc.

For information regarding special discounts for bulk purchases, please contact Simon & Schuster Special Sales at 1-800-456-6798 or business@simonandschuster.com

Cover art by Bill Petras

Printed in the U.S.A.

To the fine men and women of the
U.S.S. Carl Vinson (CVN-70).
May God go with you as you cross the beach
and grant you calm seas on your journey home.
Vis per mare.

THE SPEED OF DARKNESS

CHAPTER 1

DOWNFALL

GOLDEN . . .

That was his word for it, that rare, perfect day that warms the soul with a golden glow of joy. There was peace in a golden day.

Some days were gray, hung with leaden clouds and rain punctuated by brilliant flashes of burning white and rolling thunder. Other days were a vibrant cold blue arching over the frost-encrusted domes and sheds of the settlement. Some days were even red— the evening sky painted by the dust in the spring winds before the crops had gotten their own hold on the soil. Some days even extended into the night with a velvety cobalt blanket across the sky.

He liked those autumn nights when he could leave his world behind by staring up into that rich darkness. God had put pinpricks in the dome of the night, he imagined, so that His light could shine through. As a child he had searched the stars, hoping to see through to the other side and catch some glimpse of this

Creator. He had never stopped looking, even though he had reached his nineteenth birthday and had thought himself too mature for such things.

Each day held different colors for him. He had experienced them in all their hues. Each held a memory and a place in his heart. Yet none in his experience could compare to a golden day. It was the color of the wheat fields that rolled like waves across the low hills stretching out from his father's homestead. Golden was the warmth of the sun on his face. Golden was the glow he felt within him.

Golden was the color of her hair and the sound of her voice.

"You're dreaming again, Ardo," she whispered playfully. "Come back to me. You are much too far away!"

He opened his eyes. She was golden.

"Melani, I'm right here." Ardo smiled.

"No, you aren't." She pouted—a formidable weapon in getting her way. "You're off dreaming again and you've left me behind."

He rolled onto his side, propping his head up on one elbow so that he could get a better look at her. She was just a year younger than he. Her family had arrived back when Ardo was nine years old, another group in a long line of religious refugees that fell from the sky to join with other Saints in Helaman Township.

Refugee survivors had been gathering from nearly all the planets of the Confederacy back then—reluctant pioneers of the stars. Many devout religious groups had been among the first to be outlawed by the United Powers League on Earth back in '31. It was not a new story to Saints and Martyrs. Throughout humanity's history, those who did not understand the faithful had driven them from place to place and home to home. That they should be driven from planet to planet, then star to star, was beginning to sound painfully repetitious in their Heritage classes. Now, exiles once more, families of the faithful were scattered among the ill-fated transports of the ATLAS project, and when that mission ended in such cataclysmic failure, those families who survived searched desperately for their brothers and sisters. When communication was finally established between worlds, the Patriarchs chose an outlying region on a world they called Bountiful for their new home. Soon, Orbital Dropships were landing at the Zarahemla Starport daily. The newly arrived families would then make their way to the outlying settlements as best they could. Arthur and Keti Bradlaw, with their wide-eyed daughter, were one of five families that arrived that day. Ardo had joined his father as the entire township came out to welcome the new families and get them settled.

Ardo could not remember much about Melani then, although he had been vaguely aware of the stick of a girl who seemed awkward, lonely, and shy. He first took real notice of her when her fourteenth year brought some rather remarkable changes. The "stick

girl" seemed to burst into his awareness like a butter-
fly unfolding from its chrysalis. Her features held a
natural beauty—body painting and makeup were
frowned upon by the Patriarchs of the township—and
it had been Ardo's great good fortune to have been
the first to approach her. His heart and soul fell into
her large, luminescent blue eyes.

The nimbus of her long, shining hair played softly
in the warm breeze drifting over the wheat fields. The
wind carried the distant hum of the mill and the faint
scent of the bread at the bakery.

Golden.

"I may be off dreaming, but I'll never leave you
behind," he said to her, smiling. The wheat rustled
about the blanket where they lay. "Tell me where you
want to go. I'll take you there!"

"Right now?" Her laugh was sunshine. "In your
dreams?"

"Sure!" Ardo pulled himself up to kneel on the
heavy blanket he had spread out for them.
"Anywhere in the stars!"

"I can't go anywhere." She smiled. "I have a test in
Sister Johnson's Hydroponics class this afternoon!
Besides," she said more earnestly. "Why would I want
to go anywhere else at all? Everything I want is right
here."

Golden. Who could ever leave on such a golden
day?

"Then let's not go anywhere," he said eagerly.
"Let's stay here . . . and get married."

"Married?" She looked at him, half bemused and half questioning. "I told you, I have Hydroponics class this afternoon."

"No, I mean it." Ardo had been working himself up for this for some time. "I've graduated, and things are working out really well on Dad's agraplots. He said he was thinking of giving me forty acres at the far end of the homestead. It's the sweetest place, right up near the base of the canyon. There's a spot there next to the river where . . . where . . . Melani?"

The girl with the golden hair did not hear him. She sat up, her blue eyes squinting toward the township. "The siren, Ardo!"

Then he heard it, too. The distant wail, rising and falling across the fields.

Ardo shook his head. "They always sound it at noon . . ."

"But it *isn't* noon, Ardo."

The sun was eclipsed in that instant. Ardo leaped up, wheeling around toward the darkened sky. His mouth fell open as the lengthening shadow surged across the yellowed fields of wheat. Ardo's eyes went wide with the rush of fear. Adrenaline roared into his veins.

Enormous plumes of smoke trailed behind fireballs roaring directly toward him from the western end of the broad valley. Ardo quickly reached down and pulled Melani to her feet. His mind raced. They had to run, find shelter . . . But where could they go? Melani screamed, and he realized that there was nowhere to go and noplace safe to hide.

The fireballs seemed so close that both of them ducked. The flames arched over them, the thunderous sound of their fury quickly drowning the distant warning siren. The shadow of their wake covered the entire valley. Five enormous columns crossed overhead, their fingers reaching over Ardo and Melani toward the clustered buildings of Helaman Township. Then the fireballs wheeled as one, lifted over the township, and descended in roiling flames into Segard Yohansen's instantly ruined fields, about a mile past the center of Helaman.

Ardo shook—whether from fear or excitement he could not tell—but at least his stupor had ended. He clasped Melani's arm and began pulling at her. "Come on! We've got to get into the town before they shut the gates! Come on!"

She needed no further urging.

They ran.

He could not remember how they got into town.

The golden day had turned a muddy brown fading to gray from the smoke that still coated the sky overhead. It was an oppressive color, slate and cold. It seemed so out of place here.

"We've got to find my Uncle Dez," he heard himself say. "He has a shop in the compound! Come on! Come on!"

Ardo and Melani struggled to move through the center of the township, now crowded with refugees. Helaman originally had been nothing but an outpost in the far reaches of Bountiful. Its town center was the original fortress compound with the defensive wall encompassing the main buildings. Since then, the town had grown well beyond those central walls. Now more than ten thousand people called Helaman their home—and nearly all of them had poured into the safety of the old fortress compound.

He could just see the sign "Dez Hardwarez" across the packed central square.

The rattle of automatic weapons clattered suddenly from the perimeter wall. Two dull explosive thuds resounded, followed by even more chattering machine guns.

A cry arose from the crowd in the square. Ardo felt more than heard the fear in the seething mob. Shouts rang out, some strident and others calming. The smoke overhead cast an oppressive veil over the surging mob.

"Please, Ardo!" Melani said, "I . . . Where do we go? What do we do?"

Ardo glanced around. He could taste the panic in the air.

"We just need to get across the square," he choked out, then, seeing the look in her eyes. "We've done it hundreds of times."

"But, Ardo—"

"It isn't any farther than it was before. Just a little more crowded, that's all." Ardo looked at the tears welling up in those beautiful blue eyes. He squeezed her hand tightly. "Don't worry. I'll be right here with you."

Somehow, they were halfway across the square when it came.

A sheet of flame erupted beyond the fortress's outer wall. Its crimson light flashed against the blanket of smoke that hung oppressively over the town. The blood-red hue electrified the panicked crowd in the square. Screams, shouts, and cries all tumbled into a cacophony of sound, but several disembodied voices penetrated Ardo's thoughts clearly.

"Where are the Confederacy forces? Where are the Marines?"

"Don't argue with me! Get the children! Stay together!"

"It can't be the Zerg! They couldn't have penetrated so far into the Confederacy . . ."

Zerg? Ardo had heard rumors about them. Nightmares, so he thought, to scare children or keep outsiders from settling in the Outer Colonies. He could not remember all the whispered tales, but the nightmare was here now, and very real.

Another voice penetrated his thoughts. He turned toward her.

"Ardo, I'm frightened!" Melani's eyes were wide and liquid. "What is it? What's going on?"

Ardo opened his mouth. He could not answer her question. No words came out. There were so many words he wanted to say to her in that moment—so many words that he would regret never having said for uncounted years to come. But no words came out.

A light flared. He felt the heat on his back. He turned, holding Melani behind him.

The eastern wall had been breached. The old rampart was being pulled down from the other side, dismantled before Ardo's eyes. It seemed as though a dark wave was breaking against the breach, an undulating silhouette. Then details lodged in his mind: a gleaming purple carapace, red-streaked ivory claws sliding from a colonist's limp body, the arching, snakelike bodies writhing across the broken stone.

It was unthinkable. . . . The nightmare had come to Bountiful.

The shoulder-to-shoulder crowd in the square roared their deep fear and turned to run from the breach. There was nowhere to go. Zerg Hydralisks had already crested the opposite wall, cascading into the street like black drops from a greasy spill. Within moments, hideous cobralike hoods had unfolded above their razor-sharp talons. They arched their tails upward. Armored spikes exploded from their serrated shoulder sockets and darted with deadly effect into the western edge of the crowd.

Those facing the new threat suddenly tried to reverse direction, crushing back into the surging crowd behind them.

Ardo heard Melani gasp behind him. "I can't . . . I can't breathe . . ."

The mob was crushing them. Ardo looked desperately around him, trying to find a way out.

Movement overhead caught his eye. A bloated,

bulbous form like a disembodied brain drifted over the colony wall. Tendrils hung like viscera beneath it, quivering with activity. It was reaching down for the center of the crowd. Ardo had heard tales in which the Zerg had captured colonists and taken them alive to a fate that could only be worse than death.

Tears flooded Ardo's eyes. There was nowhere to go and nothing left to do.

Suddenly the Zerg Overlord drifting above the colony shuddered and slid sideways. Several explosions erupted from the side of the hideous beast. The Overlord exploded in an enormous fireball. The Zerg Hydralisks entering the compound suddenly hesitated.

A wing of five Confederacy Wraith fighters ripped through the smoke overhead, the scream of their engines nearly drowning out the cries of the terrified crowd below. Twenty-five-millimeter burst lasers pulsed repeatedly as the Wraiths wheeled through the air, the bolts slamming against targets on the far side of the crumbling fortress wall.

One of the Wraiths wavered suddenly, then exploded under a hail of ground fire from the outraged Zerg.

The Zerg who had entered the compound were pressing their attack, killing some and dragging others off without apparent distinction. They had corralled the humans; now all they had to do was harvest them from the edges of the crowd inward.

A second flight of Wraiths tore through the smoke-blackened sky. Then a single Confederacy Dropship ripped through the air, spinning in a rapid breaking maneuver and descending toward the square. The downblast from the engines created an instant hurricane on the ground. Trees bent over nearly double. It was impossible to hear anything over the roar of the engines. People all about Ardo tumbled to the ground, shielding themselves from the gale.

Ardo blinked through the dust. The Dropship continued to hover but managed somehow to lower its transport ramp into the square. He could see the silhouetted figure of a Confederacy Marine beckoning to them.

Everyone else in the square saw the Marine also. Mindlessly they charged the ramp. A human tide pulled Ardo along.

He lost Melani's hand.

"Melani!" he screamed. He tried to fight against the crushing press of the panicked crowd. His words were lost in the roar of the Dropship's engines. "Melani!"

He saw her behind him. The Zerg were pressing their attack with anger now. The Dropship was depriving them of their prize. Ardo was appalled at how quickly the large crowd had been sundered—harvested like blood-red wheat in the field. The Zerg were already nearly at Melani's side.

Ardo clawed and fought. He screamed.

Three Hydralisks grasped Melani at once, dragging her back from the edge of the crowd.

"Please, Ardo!" she wept. "Don't leave me alone!"

The mindless mob pushed him farther into the ship.

Zerg claws suddenly rang against the sides of the Dropship. The pilot had played out all the time his luck would afford. The ship responded instantly to his command, lurching upward away from the Zerg and bearing Ardo away from his home, his life, and his love.

"Don't leave me alone!" Those were her last words to him, pounding through his mind and soul, louder and louder, threatening to burst his skull . . .

Ardo's world went black. It would stay black for a very long time.

CHAPTER 2

MAR SARA

"ALL RIGHT, YOU RAW MEAT! HANG ON TO YOUR asses! We're takin' the long fall!"

Private Ardo Melnikov did not bother to glance at the sergeant as he barked at them. The man was a tic—temporarily in command—for this drop. Odds were that Ardo would never see the man once they were down. It was best to just stay out of the man's way until Ardo's new platoon was sorted out for the mission. He could barely hear the tic above the screaming engines of the Dropship and the thunder of their hot descent buffeting the hull. There was just something about the sergeant that seemed to require a full voice and an angry eye. In any event, it really did not matter to Ardo—the sergeant was just baby-sitting them down to the surface. Once he got there, Ardo knew there would be someone who would make his life miserable on a more permanent basis.

Ardo shrugged his shoulders, trying to lift his back

away from the wall pad. The interior of the Dropship was normally a hot box, but most especially during the plunge down through the atmosphere. This particular Dropship was at least two cooling units shy of keeping everyone comfortable. Now a growing patch of sweat was sticking his shoulder blades to the non-porous cushion. Sweat beaded up on his face and occasionally dropped down the front of his fatigues. The restraining bar prevented him from finding any relief from the pooling discomfort gathering at various junction points of his uniform.

Worse yet, the Dropship was fully loaded—packed shoulder to shoulder and bulkhead to bulkhead. The heat was not nearly so oppressive as the growing smell that was overwhelming the air scrubbers.

There was nothing for him to look at except the same slack and blank faces of the other Marine recruits strapped against the bulkhead across from him. There was nothing for him to listen to except the sergeant's occasional growl and the uniform roar of the hull behind him. There was nothing for him to do but wait it out with his own thoughts . . . and that was the last thing he wanted.

They haunted him, those thoughts lurking at the back of his mind. It seemed to him sometimes that the ghosts pursued him from inside his own head. Closing his eyes never banished those specters. No sound could drown them out for long. Those ghosts were all painfully bright and beautiful, terrible and crushing. They would wait quietly, patiently at the edge of his conscious thought, kept at bay by his will alone. Sometimes he would be arrogant enough to think he had them mastered and banished once and for all. Then some smell of ripening grass or plowed earth would waft past him on a breeze, or a glint of the color of light honey, or a distant whispered laugh, or some indefinable quality of his surroundings, and the demons would rush back, overwhelming him.

He would have bled tears just at the thought of them if he could.

All he wanted was to fight. He needed to fight. It was the only thing that really kept the demons at bay. He could concentrate on the mission and its objectives . . . or at least those minor objectives that his commander deemed necessary for him to know. Grand strategy was not his purview. It was none of his business. His job was to do whatever he was told to do and with as little thought as necessary. That suited him just fine.

The howling of the Dropship was tapering off. The vehicle had finally spent its energy against the atmosphere of whatever world they were plunging toward. The engines were doing their best now to make the ship imitate the grace of a bird in flight. Ardo chuckled to himself at the thought. The Quantradyne APOD-33 was the Confederacy's proof to the stars that anything with a big enough engine would fly— no matter how badly. Of course, he had made many training jumps before. Each was completely unremarkable and he really did not care to recall them in any detail.

Why reflect on something so painful as time to be still and think?

Better to concentrate on something else . . . anything else. Ardo began scanning the faces of the Marines around him. It was an exercise in self-preservation. It was always a good idea to know the Marines around you. You never knew when your life might depend on one of them . . . or be threatened by one.

The woman sitting across from him seemed to be a good example of one kind or the other—it was just that Ardo was not all that sure of which. She had close-cropped blond hair that stood in neat bristles from a well-shaped scalp. Her face was drawn tight, with angular cheekbones that sharply framed two shining, steel-tinged eyes. They stared unfocused at some distant point past Ardo's shoulder, unblinking yet shuttered windows into any soul she might possess. *Those eyes could freeze a river solid in midsummer,* he thought. He was left to his own imagination as to what the rest of her looked like. The powered combat suit she wore effectively hid any physical distinction she might otherwise have displayed, but it did tell him one thing: her suit markings were that of an officer.

That meant danger to a private no matter how you cut it. Avoidance of an officer is the first thing a private learns—especially in casual conversation. The last private he could remember being too familiar with his squad leader ended up with a hole where his head had been.

The female officer had not said a word since they boarded the Dropship. She was perfectly welcome to let her silence continue as far as Ardo was concerned. *Speak when spoken to,* he thought. *Otherwise, do not go looking for trouble.*

At least *she* was comfortable, Ardo thought. Her suit was self-cooling, and he could see the power umbilical plugged into the Dropship's power bus. Ardo suspected that her chill went well beyond the physical. Someday he, too, would learn the intricate skills necessary to wear the CMC-300—maybe even the new 400 model. That day was a long way off, of course. Still, it would be a lot better to wear in combat than a few layers of ablative cloth and one's standard-issue underwear. If he could just manage to live long enough to get a combat suit of his own, his prospects would improve considerably.

Well, hopefully they would at least give him some training in a weapon. He had not even had the chance to do that yet.

The rest of the compartment was filled with grunts just like himself. Each of them wore the standard-issue detached look of a Confederacy Security Marine. Each of them dripped Confederacy sweat through their Confederacy fatigues, as was their duty.

Ardo's eye fell for a time, however, on one particularly large private. The man was enormous—Ardo remembered the prep crew had some trouble getting his harness to lock closed—and he would not stop his incessant yammering for a moment. Ardo could not imagine where they had found a uniform that would fit him. He was dark complexioned, and Ardo vaguely recalled the ancient United Powers League back on Earth had once qualified the man as "South Seas Islander." He had broad, angular features and full lips. His hair was a long mane that flowed back from his forehead and down his neck in natural black waves. The giant was gung-ho certifiable—one of those all-for-the-wall, eat-their-hearts-for-breakfast psychotics who was the first person you would want to come and pull you out of the fire and the last person you would want to follow into one.

"Get this junkwad on the ground!" The giant laughed beneath his bright eyes. "I've got some death to deal out! Want to roast me some Zerg on a spit! Maybe eat their brains straight off!"

The islander threw his head back and laughed too loudly once more. He slapped his massive hands down on the thighs of the two Marines sitting next to him. They both winced so hard from the impact that tears pooled in their eyes.

"We'll eat them for dinner, eh? Big Zerg feast! Ha! Just put this flying trashyard on the ground before I open it myself!"

The pilot in the sealed cockpit forward of the drop-bay could not possibly have heard the request but seemed willing just the same to accommodate it. The ship pivoted noticeably—Ardo knew this was a standard clearing maneuver just before landing—and the engines whined a little differently. A final bump, and the engines suddenly spindled down.

The lieutenant in front of Ardo wasted no time unplugging herself from the Dropship power, managing to get herself free before the restraining bar had lifted completely out of the way. A deft move with her free hand brought her duffel bag down from the overhead racks. She was already moving toward the ramp as it began lowering at the back of the ship. She even beat the islander, who seemed to be in his own hurry to get into whatever fight he could either find or manufacture.

Ardo took his time, tugging at his fatigues to pull them free of each of the places sweat had stuck them to his body. He could smell the change in the atmosphere already blowing in through the open ramp. An achingly dry breeze swept the musty dampness out of the compartment like a furnace. He pulled his own duffel bag from the racks and followed the others as they straggled out the back of the Dropship.

"Get your asses out here, ladies," the sergeant snarled. "We haven't got all day!"

The air was oven-hot and dry—drier than Ardo ever remembered breathing. A stiff breeze carried the furnace heat around him. His sweat evaporated almost at once as he stepped onto the tarmac of the spaceport.

Ardo glanced grimly around.

He had stepped into hell.

The world was a rusting red, colored by the sand that seemed to add its own tint to every building and vehicle regardless of its original color. The effect was all the more enhanced by the flaming dawn just breaking over the starport . . .

Or what was left of the starport. Nearly half of the seven launch control towers originally scattered around the sprawling installation were on fire. Two of them were crested only with broken rubble. Columns of smoke from various other fires could be seen rising from buildings of the starport itself. More telling, larger columns could be seen rising from the central city district of the colony several miles beyond.

It was then that Ardo heard the sound—an all too familiar sound. Drifting toward him on the breeze, he heard the cries, the anguish, the panic.

He turned sharply. On the opposite side of the field, just short of the embarkation pads, he could see the cordon of Marines surrounding the Confederacy section of the starport and the panicked mob beyond.

No!

The memories flooded over him. He stood in the colony square once more. The sounds of it filled his mind. Their cries . . . *her* cries . . .

"Don't leave me alone!" she wept.

Someone shoved Ardo hard from behind. His training took over, and he tumbled deftly before rising quickly to his feet, his hands prepared to defend and attack.

"Quit stalling, you maggot-wipe," the drop sergeant snapped. "What are you waiting for—an official welcome? Get over to the barracks for training. You're needed on the double!"

Ardo dreaded the barracks more than any other thing in his life. There was something about them that repulsed him, that shook him to his very soul whenever he just heard the word. Ardo was slightly dazed, but he knew better even as he said, "No, Sergeant, I can't . . ."

The sergeant simply knocked him down again.

"Welcome to Mar Sara, Marine! Now move!"

He moved. Gathering up his kit, Ardo joined the rest of the group from his Dropship as they made their way toward the barracks at the edge of the tarmac. He had the distinct impression of swimming against the current: everyone else on the base was moving out toward the pads. "Looks like we're the cleanup crew," Ardo muttered to himself, trying not to think about the inevitability of what was coming next. He kept his eyes to the ground, refusing to look at the box-like mobile barracks unit even as he was walking up into its interior. He looked up only when he was inside, standing with the others in rough rows in the cramped deployment room at the top of the access ramp.

The tic was still there with them, mothering them with his unique touch every step of the way. "You know the drill, boys and girls. Drop your gear and strip . . . then right back here, people!"

Ardo felt a wave of nausea wash over him. There was nothing he hated more than the barracks and there was nothing in the barracks he hated more than what they were about to force on him. He told himself that it was all part of the job, but it did not make the fact of it any less revolting to him.

Ardo herded into the adjoining barracks room—like cattle into a slaughter chute, he thought, shuddering—and found an empty bunk. Whoever had called this place home ahead of him had apparently left in a hurry. Odd bits of trash remained strewn about the bedding and the floor. Ardo thought that the tic outside probably would not have approved of such sloppy behavior. With a sigh, the young Marine began peeling off his sweat-stained shirt. He tried not to notice the others around him as they undressed. There were both men and women present—the Confederacy Marines were perfectly willing to allow both sexes to die for their missions—but Ardo was always deeply ashamed of being naked in front of men, let alone women. Young and inexperienced, he found it achingly upsetting every time he was so casually required to strip, and more than once he had been the source of considerable amusement to the other Marines.

Ardo shivered as he stepped back into the deployment room. The dry heat was rapidly cooling the sweat still on his back. He felt physically sick. He knew what was coming next.

He tried to distract himself by glancing at the others

around the room. He would barely admit to himself that his motives in doing so were more than a little tainted with puerile curiosity. The majority of those present were men, he noted—in fact, an unusually high number. He had even briefly wondered what that lieutenant would look like once taken out of her battle armor. Ardo was somewhat surprised to note that she was not among them. Was she somehow exempt from this indignity?

Two large guards with stunners were standing next to the tic. Between them, a single hatchway led into the darkened room beyond. Ardo closed his eyes, trying to calm down. The tic was reading from a hand display.

". . . Alley . . . Bounous . . ."

Ardo could not think for the pounding in his head.

". . . Mellish . . . Melnikov . . ."

Ardo took several steps forward at the sound of his name and then froze. His feet refused to move any closer to the terrifying, darkened doorway. His eyes locked on the passage beyond. Rows of man-size tubes, each filled with a blue-green liquid, lined each side of the passageway.

"Melnikov, what the hell . . . ?"

They would pack him in one of those tubes and as soon as they did the nightmare would begin.

"Melnikov!"

It was like a coffin . . . a nightmare in a coffin.

He could not move. The two guards had seen it many times before. They stepped forward casually and, as roughly as possible, helped Ardo into the darkness.

He was falling and there was no end. He did not know how he had gotten here. Was he here at all or was he somewhere else . . . someone else? He struggled to concentrate on the images and memories that were drifting past his mind, but he could not find a way to grasp them. He would reach for them, desperate to examine them, but they would fall apart like bubbles of air under water as he tried to hold them.

Bubbles of air . . .

He could breathe the water. The long clear tube was filled with the breathable water. He had tried to be brave, really he had, but in the end he had panicked and screamed and disgraced himself. They did not care, for they had seen it a thousand thousand times before. Their rough hands clamped the headpiece firmly on him and pushed him down into the tube and spun shut the seals. "We'll have to make an adjustment in this one," he heard one of them say. He held his breath as long as he could . . .

As long as he could . . . what?

What was he thinking? Why was he thinking?

Hair the color of wheat fields dancing in the summer sun. There was a golden day . . .

His hands slammed against the sides of the clear tube as his last gasp escaped his lungs. The implants charged suddenly in the headpiece and his mind exploded into a million shards.

Shards tumbled around him. Bubbles of shards.

Combat suit school. How could he have forgotten? His instructor was an old Marine named Carlyle. They spent weeks there perfecting his technique—or was it months? The combat suit was like an old friend. He seemed to have lived with one all his life . . .

The combat suit. Where was that? When was that? During the seminary class? There was Brother Gabittas teaching about the fall of the ancients and the sin of pride. Peace comes from within, a joyful knowledge of the pure voice of God speaking to each man. "Thou shalt not kill," he says, but he raises an AGR-14 gauss rifle in the front of the class.

"Here, Ardo," the brother says, walking to where the boy sat near the back of the classroom. He hands the 8-millimeter automatic weapon to the young boy who has not been paying attention. "Do unto others," he says as the boy takes the weapon.

The boy drifts away in the bubble but the weapon remains, smooth and seductive. Magnetic acceleration of the projectile to supersonic speeds with enormous kinetic punch utilizing a variety of jacketless slugs from depleted uranium to steel-tipped infantry rounds. Another old friend from long ago, the rifle turns itself inside out, explodes, and then reassembles into the face of his father.

"You'll always be my son," the old man says, with a single tear coursing down his cheek. The family agra-farm stretches beyond him in the sunset. "No matter where you go or what you do . . . you'll always be my son."

Am I? Will I?

Ardo was feeling better now. He had been disoriented when he first came out of the resocialization tanks, but he was clear-headed now.

He always felt better wearing his combat suit. It was an older CMC-300 model, but he didn't mind. He had been using a 300 for years now, and it fit him just fine.

Ardo stood packed shoulder to shoulder with other Marines. There were some Firebats as well as regulars in the Ready Room. In the little space he had, he checked the power connection between his gauss rifle and the combat suit. He loved that rifle; it was his weapon of choice. He had been firing a gauss rifle for nearly as many years as he had been working with the combat suit.

Ardo looked up. The "go" lamp over the exit hatch had just turned from red to green. A roar went up from the Marines as the door slid open in an instant.

He hated to leave, though.

He sure loved the barracks.

CHAPTER 3

OUT COUNTRY

ARDO WAS ONE OF A TIDE OF MARINES POURING uniformly from the barracks and into a world of chaos.

A company of Marines in power armor had formed a perimeter around the Confederacy section of the starport, cordoning off the military units. Beyond them, Ardo could see as he quick-marched across the tarmac, literally thousands of colonists pressed against the Marine line. Men, women, and children— a screaming mass of humanity—struggled desperately for a way off the planet.

Beyond them, the civilian side of the starport was in anarchy. All down the flight line, perhaps as many as a hundred orbital spacecraft were either clawing their way up from the surface or hovering in anticipation of launch. At least twice that number moved listlessly beyond the outer markers, the daylight glinting off their polished hulls. There was a sense of desperation in their movements. Control seemed to have been abandoned. Ships attempted to take off and land at will. Several transports hovered near the terminal building, searching for a place to put down, but the panicked mob would not, or could not, move out of the way. The still-burning wreckage of at least half a dozen ships lay strewn about the port complex. Those pilots still flying apparently paid them little heed. Like moths to a flame, they were drawn by the exorbitant ransoms they could charge anyone who managed to board. Fearful for the safety of themselves and their ships, they wanted to get in and out as quickly as possible.

If everyone is trying so hard to get out *of here, why did the Confederacy work so hard to get me* in *here?* Ardo wondered. The terribly uncomfortable, gnawing cold below his stomach reasserted itself. *I don't know these people. I don't even really know what world I'm on! What am I doing here?*

He knew his assigned transport—yet another Dropship—and found himself dashing toward it with two squads of Marines. Each individual knew where he or she was supposed to report. So it was that their squad formed up almost as if by some magnetic magic. Ardo found himself jogging behind that female lieutenant he had seen the day before. Next to him was the huge, dark islander in perhaps the largest powered armor suit Ardo had ever seen. He recognized it as a CMC-660 Heavy Combat Suit, complete with plasma generator tanks on the back. So the large islander was a Firebat, Ardo thought: one of those plasma flame-throwing units that were occasionally as dangerous to their operators as they were to the enemy. Several others followed as well, including a single technician in a set of light fatigues. Where was *he* going, Ardo thought. On vacation?

The roar of the Orbitals constantly lifting from the surrounding pads did not deter the enthusiasm of the Dropship pilot, nor did it entirely drown out his shrill words.

"Step right up, boys and girls, young and old!" he screeched, punching out the words in carnival-huckster style. "Come see the greatest show in the universe! See the local colonists run for their lives! See the government collapse before your very eyes! Witness feats of panic never before attempted by civilized man! Right this way!"

Ardo made his way toward the Dropship. The crackle of automatic gauss fire ripped through the air near the Marine cordon. Ardo winced, trying not to think of what it meant.

"Cutter!" the lieutenant barked when they arrived at the ramp leading into the ship.

"Ma'am!" the hulking islander piped up.

"Get these drip-dry recruits loaded in five minutes." Her command voice carried even over the din of the riot that was taking place all around them. "We've got a job to do. I'll sort them out once we get on station."

"Yes, ma'am! You heard the lady! Make a line!"

The small group fell in. Cutter begin making his

way down the line, making sure everyone had their gear set for transport.

The pilot leaned against the landing strut of the Dropship, and grinned.

"Okay, ladies!" Cutter was enjoying himself. "Take your places inside. Let's go!"

Ardo pulled up his kit and moved forward, suspiciously eyeing the nose art painted on the side of the ship. *Valkyrie Vixen?*

"That's right, friend," the pilot answered smugly. "They say once you've had a Valkyrie, you'll never ride another! You've come to the right place . . . or the wrong place, if you take my drift." The slim pilot had the most outrageous hair that Ardo had ever seen. Brilliant blue spikes radiated away from his head in sharp cones, the areas between them shaved bald with precision care. His gaunt frame seemed to radiate all arms and legs, a scarecrow in a flight suit with a mischievous smile that seemed to wind halfway around his head. "Tegis Marz is the name. I'm the Angel of Death for you boys out on the periphery. Happy to serve you. You need anything—including a proper butt-saving—and I'm the man to call."

"It's a death trap, and I'm not getting on it."

Tegis turned toward the voice coming from just down the line behind Ardo. It was the technician. Ardo could not remember seeing him on the transport down to the surface; the guy must have been here longer than that.

"I can't even look at it!" said the man in fatigues.

He had a slender build but was smooth-faced and sported his hair close-cropped. The guy was so clean he probably squeaked when he walked. "This piece of abandoned trash isn't even up to being *called* abandoned trash!"

Tegis stood away from the landing strut and growled menacingly. "You piece of dog puke! This ship is a thing of beauty! There's not another one like her in the entire fleet!"

"That's because the *rest* of the fleet is at least in *some* state of reasonable repair!"

"You take that back, Marcus!"

"In your dreams, Tegis!"

"You're getting on this ship right now!"

"Not if it was the last ship off this rock! I'd stand a better chance flapping my arms off a cliff than in that hurtling death trap. When you gonna grow up and get yourself a *real* ship?"

With an outraged cry, Tegis lunged at the technician. They tumbled to the ground, rolling as each pounded the other. Red dust kicked into the air around them as they fought; a blur of arms and legs. A pair of alley cats would have been hard-pressed to put up a more vicious fight.

Ardo stood there, dumbfounded. It was almost laughable.

Cutter waded into the fight and pulled the two combatants apart. "Mister Jans, I believe the lieutenant told you to get your gear on board. I think *now* would be a good time to do it."

The red-faced technician continued to claw the air in the direction of the Dropship pilot. Cutter gave him a strong shake that should have loosened the man's teeth.

"Wouldn't it?" Cutter reiterated.

Marcus Jans quit struggling. "Yes. I believe it would."

Cutter turned toward Tegis Marz. The tips of the pilot's hair spikes were still quivering with rage. "And don't you have a ship to fly?"

"Yeah," Tegis replied, still seething. "And a damn fine ship, too!"

"Then, respectfully, *sir*, maybe you had better go fly it," Cutter's smile was so full of teeth that it looked like he might eat the next person who disagreed with him. "I've got a reason to be here and I don't want anyone between me and where I'm going. And right now, you are standing *in my way . . . sir.*"

Tegis went slack. "I . . . I'll just get this *fine piece of machine* off the ground for you, then."

"You do that, sir. Thank you, sir," Cutter said, pushing each of them apart as he let them go. Staggering slightly, each of the former combatants found a great deal of interest in the ground at his feet as they moved off to take care of business elsewhere.

Ardo let out his breath in a sigh.

"What about you, soldier," Cutter said, turning his dark eyes toward Ardo for the first time. "You gonna get in my way?"

"No, sir," Ardo replied, regretting that he had not

managed to avoid the large islander's attention longer. "I'm definitely staying out of your way, sir."

The big man grinned again. There was something both devilishly playful and at the same time dangerous in that smile. "No, friend, I'm not a 'sir.'" The gloved hand he extended was enormous. "PFC Fetu Koura-Abi, but everyone just calls me Cutter."

"PFC Ardo Melnikov," he responded, grateful that the active feedback in his glove managed to dampen what might have otherwise been a crippling handshake. "Pleased to know you."

"You're lying," Cutter grinned malevolently.

"Almost," Ardo replied.

The big man threw his head back and laughed heartily. "Fair enough! Grab your kit. I want to get out to where I can burn something! Did you enjoy the show?"

Ardo picked up his kit and began making his way up the Dropship's ramp. "What? Oh, you mean the pilot and that tech?"

"Sure!" Cutter replied, carrying his own duffel bag easily over his shoulder with one hand. "It's always fun to watch brothers go at it. The best times I had were with my own brothers . . ."

Ardo turned. "You mean . . . those two are . . ."

"It's obvious." Cutter smiled, giving Ardo a playful shove back into the jump harness that nearly knocked the wind out of him. "You can't hide the blood between brothers."

Suddenly Cutter shuddered. Ardo could see some

dark thought pass over the big man's face. With a sudden cry, Cutter reached out and grabbed the sealing ring for Ardo's helmet, pulling the man's face near his own. "That's why I'm here, Melnikov. My own brothers are out there on this ball of red dust working the waterfarms in the Out Country. I will find them, Melnikov, or I will avenge them with hell's own fire! You understand me, Melnikov? You going to get in my way, Melnikov?"

Ardo calmly returned Cutter's twitching stare.

Eye for an eye, Ardo thought. Then, *Love them that hate you.*

"Ardo," he replied quietly. "You can call me Ardo, if you like."

Cutter's cheek muscles twitched. "What?"

"My name is Ardo. I hope you'll let me call you Cutter, because I don't think I caught your full name the first time."

Cutter relaxed his grip. A smile played on his lips. "Sure, Ardo. I like you. You can call me Cutter, friend. So, I guess you *are* behind me, eh?"

As far behind you as possible, Ardo thought, but aloud he said, "All the way, Cutter."

The hydraulics suddenly whined. The aft ramp was closing quickly. Cutter loosed his grip, regained his huge Cheshire Cat grin, and stepped back against the opposite wall. He was just struggling into his own drop harness when the lieutenant stepped back into their personnel bay.

"All right, listen up," she said in a solid alto voice.

"I am Lieutenant L. Z. Breanne. I'm your commanding officer for this mission."

"Ooh! How about that, boys, we got a mission!"

Lieutenant Breanne continued, her voice level and authoritative: "We don't have a lot of time, people. I've given our drop coordinates to the pilot and we should be on station at the LZ in about thirty minutes.

"Fifteen days ago, outland colonist stations began going silent. Initial investigations resulted in lost recon squads. A subsequent reconnaissance-in-force ten days ago confirmed that this planet has been infested with what we now call the Zerg . . ."

"Zergs, boys!" Alley smiled.

"Pardon, ma'am, but what's a Zerg?" Mellish sniffed.

"A new species of alien life-form. We don't know too much about them at this point . . ."

"Bring on the barbecue!" Cutter chattered.

Breanne ignored them for the time being. "Given the planetwide saturation of these Zerg—whatever they are—the Confederacy has determined to withdraw its assets from Mar Sara—"

"Hey, the Confederacy is hauling its 'assets' out!" Marcus snorted.

Laughter rolled around the cabin.

"Stow it, Jans, or I'll put you in a bag myself." Lieutenant Breanne meant it, and there was not a person in the compartment who thought otherwise. "Our mission is threefold: first, hold the forward bunker position at three-nine-two-seven in support of the Confederacy evacuation; second, recon enemy activity forward of that position, and, finally, pick up a little bauble that command lost along the way. That's all."

"Uh, Lieutenant," Cutter asked. "What kind of . . . bauble?"

"You'll know when I see it, Cutter," Breanne said. "On board you'll find a scanner plug-in for your armor. It has been precalibrated to acquire the target. I don't know what the target is, and you don't really care. But if we *do* find it, it's our ticket off this rock. I'll give you more once we've got the position secure. That's all."

Lieutenant Breanne turned and took her place in her own jump harness. Once again, Ardo found himself opposite the woman, now his commander.

"Begging your pardon, Lieutenant," Ardo asked. The engines of the Dropship were spinning up.

"What is it, soldier?" Breanne looked at him with those steel-cold eyes.

"You said we were here to cover the evac of the Confederacy personnel and equipment?"

"Yes, that's part of the mission," she replied over the increasing noise.

"What about the colonists?" Ardo called out over the roar. "Are we here to cover the evacuation of the colonists, too?"

If Breanne had a response, she did not bother to give it. Perhaps the engine noise was now just too great. Perhaps she simply had no answer to give him.

Ardo settled back once more into the jump harness and dreaded the next thirty minutes. He closed his eyes for a moment and could see in his mind the ruins of Mar Sara's starport receding below. Through the roar shaking the hull he could have sworn he heard the cries of the thousands below him desperate to escape.

He thought he saw Melani's face among them.

CHAPTER 4

LITTLEFIELD

ARDO FLEW OVER A WORLD OF RUST. THE SHEER faces of the distant mountains were rust. The crags that cut into the earth were rust. Even the outskirts of the settlement city were coated with a layer of rust. Only days ago, those buildings were occupied, and the fine dust that blew across the arid world was diligently kept at bay. Now the world itself was taking no time in reclaiming the surface as its own.

All of this, Ardo experienced vicariously through his combat suit. He was plugged into the Dropship's main power bus, which also transmitted to him a continuous stream of data that Ardo could configure in any way that he liked. He had switched the sensor system over to external, and instantly the ship had vanished around him. He soared above the landscape alone, the internal display system automatically masking out the Dropship around him and everyone inside it. He was a bird sailing the hot plasma fire that trailed behind him.

The outskirts of the central city fell quickly behind. Below was a wasteland, cratered and scarred black from the battles that had preceded him here. The scattered carnage of desperate struggles dotted the shattered land. The occasional hulks of Vulture hover-cycles and hundreds of civilian transports formed twisted, black-metal flower petals here and there.

Ardo sailed through the sky above it all and wondered at it. Where were the siege tanks, the mobile artillery, the Goliath assault walkers? Everything he could see below him was strictly light armaments and local militia trash.

More important, where were they deploying if the battle below had already been lost? Ardo looked ahead. His flight was slowing as he descended toward an outpost bunker complex and the landing zone just inside its perimeter.

"Get your head out, Marine," the sharp voice of Lieutenant Breanne sounded through his com-system. "It's time to disembark."

The Dropship materialized around him almost at once as his attention shifted. The lieutenant was staring coolly into his faceplate.

"Yes, ma'am," Ardo responded sharply. "Ready, ma'am!"

Lieutenant Breanne gave no more acknowledgment than a moment's look into Ardo's eyes and then turned to address the squad. Her voice cut across the whine of the engines. "We're here for a reason, boys and girls! Let's get the job done and get out. Is that clear?"

"Ma'am! Yes, ma'am!" they all barked as one.

"You have ten minutes from touchdown to find your bunk and stow your gear. You will then report to me outside the command bunker for immediate deployment." Lieutenant Breanne extended two fingers together as she indicated the Marines around her. "Cutter, Wabowski, both of you will prep Firebat cat-five. The rest of you prep for recon-in-force, cat-three configuration."

Ardo ran through the category-3 checklist in a moment: power armor, Impaler gauss rifle with infantry loads, no field pack . . . fast on their feet and ready for anything. It also meant they would not be going too far from the encampment. Sounded like a pleasant afternoon after all.

Lieutenant Breanne paused a moment as she looked down the bay, filled with the members of her squad. Ardo wondered what the lieutenant was thinking.

"Be a minute late, you won't be breathing after two. Clear?"

"Ma'am! Yes, ma'am!"

The Dropship lurched suddenly, landing hard. The lieutenant snatched a handhold instantly, then snapped shut her suit visor.

She had cleared the lowering exit ramp before it even touched the ground.

*   *   *

Ardo tried to move through the barracks hatch, but he felt so confused. He couldn't seem to concentrate very well on even simple tasks. His duffel bag got caught somewhere on the other side of the frame as he tried to enter the barracks. His face flushed red from the tittering laughter that rolled around the double rows of bunks. It spurred him to try harder, but his anger and embarrassment just managed somehow to keep him from turning the bag the right way. His mind seemed caught in some kind of a terrible loop—understanding what he was doing wrong but somehow not being able to correct it.

"Easy, soldier," said an older Marine from his top bunk. "Let me give you a hand with that."

"Don't trouble yourself, mister," Ardo grumbled. Some part of him was sure the old man just meant to embarrass him further.

The older Marine snorted, then rolled out of his bunk. "Look, kid, it's no trouble at all. Sometimes you just gotta let things slack off a little and they work themselves out. You're just trying too hard."

The Marine gently rested his hand on Ardo's arm.

Ardo snatched back his arm angrily. The power armor protected his elbow as it slammed against the metal wall and left a rather sizable dent, but the shock of it numbed his arm. The duffel bag fell with a jumbled clank to the floor.

The older Marine shook his head and smiled. Ardo could barely see the man through his own dizzying pain and embarrassment. He had iron-gray hair in long, unkempt strands, and the faint grizzle of a beard. Piercing dark eyes looked out of a scarred and twisted face. Ardo guessed that the man was in his late thirties, although the ravages of his face made that only a guess. That twisted face continued to smile at Ardo, however, putting his two hands up in front of him, palms out, in a sign of surrender. Then, slowly, the man reached through the hatchway, drew the bag into the compartment, and set it down in front of Ardo.

"Easy, brother," he said. "Looks like you're fresh out of the resoc tank. They can scramble your head up pretty good for a while."

Ardo merely nodded sullenly. The electric feeling was subsiding in his elbow.

"Jon Littlefield," the Marine said as he extended his large, callused hand. "Glad to meet you, brother."

Ardo blinked. Something in the back of his mind screamed at him from a distance, but he could not understand what it was saying. The thought of being called "brother" somehow made him dizzy.

The memories bounded and rebounded within his mind in a bewildering cascade.

"Brother Melnikov!" His youth leader smiled brilliantly in the dawning light . . .

His father's voice: "All are brothers in God's eyes, son. Brothers do not kill brothers . . ."

"Brother?" Ardo blinked as he spoke, trying to steady himself.

"Sure." Jon sniffed. "We're all brothers here—

brothers in arms, brothers in combat. Face it, recruit, all we've got out here is each other."

Melani's receding face, twisted in horror as the Zerg dragged her bleeding to the grass of the square.

"Yes . . . of course," Ardo said, his eyes looking down at the deck. "We're all we've got."

Jon Littlefield deftly picked up the bag and tossed it onto the bunk beneath his own. "Don't you worry, son. I've been 'on the quick' for most of my life as a Marine. Stick with me, boy, and you'll do all right. We'll straighten out your head and you'll be feeling better in no time."

Ardo stared blankly at Jon Littlefield. If Littlefield was in his early thirties, then the man was old . . . older than any Marine he remembered seeing. He had seen older men before, of course, back on Bountiful. The Patriarchs of the colony were all gray-haired elders. He remembered that they all seemed so wise. It had been comforting at the time to have leaders who had survived so long. They had wisdom of their own instead of borrowed from someone else. Now that he thought about it, Littlefield was about the oldest man he had seen among the Marines who was anything less than a colonel.

"Old at thirty" was not on any of the recruiting posters.

What do I care? Ardo thought. *I didn't join up for the retirement plan. I owe the Zerg for what they did, and if I get my payback before they take me, all the better.*

Cutter deftly squeezed his enormous frame

through the hatch. His bulk nearly filled the space between Ardo and Littlefield.

"Well, Sergeant Littlefield!" Cutter's sarcasm and disdain were evident in his tone as he looked down on the older Marine. "Wasn't that *Captain* Littlefield when we last served together, *sir?*"

Ardo was shocked for a moment that a private would be so disrespectful of an officer, even a non-commissioned one.

Jon apparently chose to simply ignore the obvious insult as he smiled back his response. "It's nice to see you in my squad, Private. You'd all better get on the quick now. Lieutenant Breanne has a bee up her butt and won't stop until she's spilled a little blood on one side or the other. You've got the config, so let's get prepped and get out!"

CHAPTER 5

MISSION ELAPSED TIME

THE WIND WHIPPED ACROSS THE CRAGGY, DESO-late landscape. Ardo could almost feel the grains of sand digging into the joints of his Powered Combat Suit. There was no help for it. The squad was at attention. If he even contemplated making a move, Ardo felt sure that Lieutenant Breanne would make it his last.

Even though the combat suit carefully controlled his body temperature to keep it at its peak performance, he felt a rivulet of sweat start to make its way between his shoulder blades toward the hollow of his back. Maybe Sergeant Littlefield was right. Maybe something was still scrambled in his head after his resoc back at the starport. He was having a little trouble concentrating, and there was a sense of foreboding that seemed to hover just at the edge of his conscious thoughts. His father had often called such notions the "promptings of the Spirit," that still, small voice that came to men to give them divine direction. "Heed that voice," his father had said, "and it will never lead you wrong."

Where was that warning Spirit when the Zerg had torn his parents apart limb by limb?

A sharp, blinding pain shot through the back of his right eye. Ardo winced as a wave of nausea followed. The image of spraying his breakfast hash across his battlesuit visor flitted across his mind. *Littlefield said it would pass,* Ardo thought as he struggled to regain his mental balance. *Just hang on for a moment and it will be all right.*

He tried, instead, to concentrate on Lieutenant Breanne. She stood before them, the polarized field of her bubble helmet deliberately turned down so that everyone could see her face clearly as she spoke. Everyone in the squad faced rigidly forward. No one wanted to risk catching her eye as she strode before them.

"With everyone pulling out, they're sending us in, my beauties," her voice sounded before them, only slightly distorted by the helmet she wore. Aural directional enhancers in the suits made both transmitted and external sounds seem to come from the direction of their source. "The entire Confederacy force is jumping off the surface of this rock."

But what of the colonists? Ardo thought. *Is the Confederacy leaving them as well?*

"Before we join our brothers in abandoning this dustball of a planet, we've got a job to do."

"Burning to burn 'em, ma'am!" Cutter interrupted enthusiastically in a crisp, military voice.

Breanne smiled like a wolf in response. "You'll have plenty to roast with that toy of yours before we're finished, Mister Koura-Abi. I would suggest, however, that we get the present job done first and get off this rock while we still have a way out."

"Ma'am! Yes, ma'am!" Cutter sounded a little disappointed.

"Your new home—if any of you are wondering—is Bunker Complex 3847. A week ago it was an outpost settlement. Folks used to call it Scenic, God knows why. It's all ours now. Enjoy it while you can 'cause I don't intend to stay here one moment more than we have to for this mission.

"There's an old pumping settlement in the bottom of an impact crater just northeast of here. It's a collection of scrap called Oasis about three clicks out on a radial of thirty-five degrees from the command transmitter. Set your navigational transceivers to those coordinates. Captain Marz here"—the pilot stood squinting in the blowing dust, managing to wave his hand slightly in reluctant identification—"will be flying cover and directing us below."

"Flying cover?" It was Sejak, the young kid. "In a Dropship?"

"The *Vixen* has been fitted with a special receiver, Mister Sejak, to help us locate this thing we are looking for. Do you have a problem with this, mister?"

The tone in her voice should have frosted over Sejak's faceplate from the inside. "No, ma'am!"

"We find this thing, we pull out and bring it with us. Clean and quick. Corporal Smith-puun will lead First Squad on Vultures with Bowers, Fu, Peaches, and Windom. Littlefield?"

"Yes, ma'am!" The old Marine's voice sounded loud in Ardo's helmet. Littlefield was standing right next to him.

"You take Second Squad—that will be Alley, Bernelli, Melnikov, and Xiang. Cutter and Ekart will give you heavy support in the Firebats."

Ardo took in the names of his squad as best he could. Bernelli, Xiang, and Ekart were unfamiliar to him. Cutter was still a very dangerous mystery. If they needed a squad leader, though, Littlefield gave him a little more hope than he might have had otherwise.

"Ma'am! Yes, ma'am!" Littlefield barked back enthusiastically.

Breanne barely took notice. "Jensen, you're boss of Third Squad. That's Collin, Mellish, Esson, and M'butu. Wabowski gives you Firebat support."

"Yes, ma'am," Jensen replied without much enthusiasm. Ardo hoped the man fought better than he talked. He looked as though he were about to fall asleep where he stood.

"The Dropship will fly high cover and sensor support until we've got the prize. Then we dust off and get off this rock. Any questions?" When Breanne said it, it was a dare, not an invitation.

Ardo could not help himself. He stepped forward and saluted as he spoke. "Ma'am! Yes, ma'am!"

"Yes, Mister . . . Melkof, isn't it?"

"Melnikov, ma'am. Begging your pardon, ma'am!"

"What's your question, Melnikov?"

"What are we looking for, ma'am?"

Lieutenant Breanne looked away from him, her eyes focusing into the distance.

"A box, Private. Just a box."

Ardo felt wonderful. He loved running in the power armor. It seemed effortless as he bounded across the ground. The clicks rolled under him, the salmon colored dust trailing behind him and his companions.

He switched the visor of his battlesuit to navigation mode. Wherever he looked, the visor superimposed the map of their surrounding terrain and labels of the more prominent landmarks. Despite what the lieutenant had said, Scenic had been aptly named. The settlement's primary job had been to maintain the upper pumping station for the aqueduct pipes coming up out of Oasis. As such, it was situated on the sheer drop-off that marked the edge of the Basin—the remains of a major impact crater that had gouged a magnificent long bowl out of the surface. The remains of the crater rim had eroded somewhat over time. His visor labeled the razor peaks to his left as "Stonewall" and the embarrassingly appropriate peak to his left as "Molly's Nipple." The crater itself was a barren landscape, like so much of the entire world of Mar Sara, but there was a stark beauty in its ruggedness that pleased Ardo's eye.

A road snaked its way in switchbacks down the steep incline of the crater edge. Ardo smiled again at the thought of the local civvies slowly winding their tortured way down that treacherous road before reaching the valley floor. The Marines were not constrained by such weakness. His entire squad had bounded over the steep edge of the mesa and had galloped straight down to the crater floor. The battlesuits were designed to take a lot more punishment than a little tumble down a cliff face. And the Marines inside them were, he thought smartly, tougher than the suits they wore.

"Hubris . . ." It was his father's voice. *"Pride cometh before a fall . . ."*

Ardo frowned. His headache threatened suddenly to return. Better not to think about it and concentrate on his job.

First Squad floated off to his squad's right on their four hover-cycles. Normally, mobile units in siege tanks or even a pair of Goliath Walkers would supplement the platoon. Ardo rather thought that First Squad had arrived hoping for such heavy equipment. They were destined for disappointment, being issued local Vulture Hover Bikes that had recently been "liberated" from the local militia. They were fast, light, and highly maneuverable, and they gave their riders about as much protection as a paper hat. The squad leader, a corporal named Smith-puun, was having some difficulty holding back the cycles to stay even with the two other Marine squads beating feet across the floor of the crater.

Third Squad was running flank off to his left while Ardo's own Second Squad was taking point for the group. They all ran in a line, the slope of the crater floor gradually flattening out. Above them all, the *Valkyrie Vixen* howled, her downward angled jets churning a wall of dust behind the platoon's own.

Lieutenant Breanne ran slightly behind Third Squad. That was surprising. Ardo had expected the lieutenant to stay aloft in the Dropship and run the entire show from up there. He had served under other commanders who preferred to backseat-drive their platoons from a pleasantly remote location. His own estimation of Breanne went up several points.

The ground shook underfoot with each stride Ardo made. The oxygen in the suit poured into him, making him feel alive, ready and anxious to do his duty for the Confederacy.

We are tough, Ardo thought. *Everyone says so . . .* although he could not recall just who had said so or where he had heard it ever really said.

All he knew was that the outskirts of Oasis were coming up fast before him, and he would finally be able to exact justice for what the Zerg had done to him.

*   *   *

TRANSCRIPT / CONCOM417 / MET:00:04:23

LC: Lieutenant L.Z. Breanne, Commanding

3 Squads 1:a-e (Mech/Cycle); 2:a-g (M/Inf) / 3:a-f (M/Inf)

Support: DS (Dropship *Valkyrie Vixen* / Tegis Marz, Pilot)

BEGIN:

LC/BREANNE: "Okay, grunts! Time for work! First Squad, give me a circle pass on the outpost perimeter."

1A/SMITH-PUUN: ". . . again? Say again?"

LC/BREANNE: "First Squad . . . circle Oasis and report!"

1A/SMITH-PUUN: "Yeah, I got it. . . . Fu, break left and take it high, man, and stay tight. If you go buggin' out on me again, I'll cash you in this time, I swear!"

1B/BOWERS: "Yeah, I love you, too, Corporal!"

LC/BREANNE: "Second Squad, cover Third Squad at that barricade."

2A/LITTLEFIELD: "We're on it! Go!"

LC/BREANNE: "Third Squad . . ."

3B/WABOWSKI: "Hey, we're already there, lady!"

LC/BREANNE: ". . . move up and recon the . . . Cutter, you'll wait for my command or I'll be tacking your hide up on my office wall!"

3A/JENSEN: "Roger, Lieutenant! We are at the breach."

MET: 00:04:24

3C/COLLINS: "Hey, Sarge! What is this stuff? It's all over the ground!"

3B/WABOWSKI: "That's Zerg shit, Ekart. They spread this crap all over the place when they come through."

2E/ALLEY: "Lordy, that's nasty! Looks like them bugs just coated the whole town with their black vomit!"

2A/LITTLEFIELD: "Shut up, Alley . . . and keep your field of fire clear! The way you're wavin' that rifle around, you'd think you were conducting a parade!"

MET: 00:04:25

2E/ALLEY: "I'm watching their back, Sarge. Don't get your panties . . ."

3A/JENSEN: "Lieutenant, this is Jensen. I'm at the breach. There's a lot of Zerg creep in here. There's got to be a colony nearby."

1A/SMITH-PUUN: "That's bullshit, Lieutenant! We've just made our circuit and there's no hive here."

1B/BOWERS: "Yeah, you tell 'em, Smith-puun!"

3A/JENSEN: ". . . all you want, Corporal, but this is Hive creep and it's flowed down the length of the main street and around the buildings. I can't tell where it's coming from."

1A/SMITH-PUUN: "That's 'cause it ain't coming from anywhere, Jensen! I'm tellin' ya there . . ."

MET: 00:04:26

LC/BREANNE: "Knock it off, Smith-puun. Jensen, any contact?"

3A/JENSEN: "Just this creep, Lieutenant. Otherwise, negative."

LC/BREANNE: "Very well. Marz, how about it? Is there . . ."

1A/SMITH-PUUN: "Fu, I'm tellin' you for the last time, take that cycle higher. Windom! Tighten it up, will ya? And watch out for those aqueducts! You hit one of those and it will ruin your whole day!"

DS/VALKYRIE: "Say again, Lieutenant?"

LC/BREANNE: "Any sign of what we're looking for?"

MET: 00:04:26

DS/VALKYRIE: "Negative, Lieutenant. Sensor's still clear. No indication yet. I think you're getting too much interference from the buildings. You'll have to get . . ."

1B/BOWERS: "That close enough for you, Smith-puun, or do you want me to ride your cycle for you?"

LC/BREANNE: "Shut up, Bowers! Marz, say again?"

DS/VALKYRIE: "Your squads have to get closer. Send 'em in."

2E/ALLEY: "In there? You gotta be kiddin' me!"

LC/BREANNE: "Roger, Marz. Second Squad, move up. Third Squad . . ."

2A/LITTLEFIELD: "Roger . . . moving up."

LC/BREANNE: ". . . and recon eastern buildings up to the . . ."

3A/JENSEN: "Say again? Say again?"

LC/BREANNE: "I said spread your squad out and recon the eastern buildings up to the transmission tower. Second Squad, you . . ."

1B/BOWERS: "There's nothin' out here, Smith-puun! We're just burning circles in the air."

1A/SMITH-PUUN: "Be grateful, Bowers, 'cause if there *was* anything out here . . ."

LC/BREANNE: "Keep the chatter off the command channel! Second Squad, you take the western side. Make your way between the condensers and circle around to the administration center!"

MET: 00:04:27

2A/LITTLEFIELD: "Roger. We're on it. Sejak, you go with Mellish and check out the condensers. The rest of you come with me."

3A/JENSEN: "You all heard the lady, let's move! Cutter, you follow Alley and Xiang up the main street here. Ekart, you're with Melnikov and Bernelli. Go right down that road and then make your way north toward the . . ."

1D/PEACHES: "Hey, Smith-puun! Did you see that?"

1A/SMITH-PUUN: "You heard the lady, Windom. Cut the chatter . . ."

1D/PEACHES: "Something's moving down there!"

1A/SMITH-PUUN: "Where?"

1B/Bowers: "There's nothin' moving, I tell ya!"

Met: 00:04:28

3D/Mellish: "Sarge? Can we walk on this—this creepy stuff?"

3A/Jensen: "It's called creep, Melnikov. Yeah, you can walk on it. It looks wet, but it's probably harder than your power armor."

2A/Littlefield: "Keep moving those sensors around, ladies. The sooner we find this thing, the sooner we get back for chow."

1E/Windom: "Peaches is right, Corp, there's something moving down there."

1B/Bowers: "You're seeing things, Windom!"

1D/Peaches: "No, I see it, too. Over by the com tower, in the shadows!"

LC/Breanne: "Let's get this over with and get out. Marz, anything yet?

Met: 00:04:29

DS/Valkyrie: "Not yet, Lieutenant . . . keep 'em moving."

2D/Melnikov: "Hey, I think I'm getting something here . . ."

LC/Breanne: "Melnikov . . . what is it?"

2D/Melnikov: "Sarge, I think you need to take a look at this."

2A/Littlefield: "Where are you, Melnikov?"

Met: 00:04:30

2A/Littlefield: "Melnikov, say again. Where are you?"

LC/Breanne: "Littlefield, what's going on?"

2A/LITTLEFIELD: "Ekart, where's Melnikov?"

2G/EKART: "I'm not the kid's baby-sitter, Sarge."

2A/LITTLEFIELD: "Ekart, answer me."

2G/EKART: "Look, he was behind me a minute ago!"

2A/LITTLEFIELD: "Bernelli?"

2C/BERNELLI: "He's just around the corner, Sarge."

2A/LITTLEFIELD: "Can you see him?"

2C/BERNELLI:"Well, he's just . . . Hey, where did he go?"

MET: 00:04:31

LC/BREANNE: "Melnikov, report!"

MET: 00:04:32

LC/BREANNE: "Melnikov! *Report!*"

CHAPTER 6

RABBIT HOLE

ARDO FELL.

There was a timelessness about his fall, a descent into blackness that seemed never to end. His helmet slamming against the unseen sides of the dark shaft punctuated his freefall. His arms and legs wrenched and twisted with impact from time to time but were saved from serious damage by the automatic safety servos of the battle armor. Still he fell, farther and farther into the unknowable blackness beneath him.

He landed with a shock, rubble cascading around him as he slammed facedown against the hard floor of the shaft. The suit had saved his life, reacting automatically to his descent, but now the broken and collapsing edges of the shaft overhead tumbled down around him, burying him deep in the bowels of a world that was not his own.

Panic gripped him. He screamed: a scream that rattled weak and hollow in his own ears despite its rebounding within his helmet. He thrashed his arms and legs wildly against the debris, kicking at the dark objects rolling about him. He staggered to his feet, losing his balance in his haste and falling backward once more, his arms and legs flailing as he tried to find some purchase. His back slammed against the smooth wall behind him. There, his quivering legs beneath him at last, he stood leaning against the wall, gulping air and trying desperately to regain control of himself.

Darkness surrounded him, complete and utter.

Ardo shuddered, struggling against his quick and shallow breaths. *"Take a deep breath, Ardo," his mother said, concern in her eyes. "Don't say anything until you've taken a deep breath."*

He sucked in a shivering breath.

"Melnikov to . . . Melnikov to . . . Cutter!" It took him a moment to remember the name. "Cutter . . . Come in, Cutter!"

Only faint hissing sounded in his ears.

Ardo took another hesitant deep breath.

"Ekart? . . . Bernelli? Can you . . . can you read me? Come in, Ekart! Bernelli! I've fallen down a shaft at . . ."

At where? The heads-up display of his visor was blank. The navigational display was flashing LOS, which meant it was no longer in contact with the navigational beacon back at the base. How far *had* he fallen, anyway? He remembered that he had been walking along on top of the creep, sweeping down the east side toward the tower.

Ardo's breath froze. The creep!

Instinctively, he leveled the muzzle of his gauss rifle in front of him with his right hand. His left hand reached down behind him to feel along the wall at his back. The powered glove of the battlesuit slid smoothly along the ribbed, slick surface.

"*Damn!*" he breathed, eyes suddenly wide with fear.

Ardo gripped the gauss rifle with both hands, pushing himself away from the wall. He leaned slightly forward into the rifle as he had been trained to do. "Light! Full spectrum!"

The helmet-mounted illuminators suddenly flashed brightly to life.

The Zergling was at least ten meters down the spore colony tunnel that appeared immediately to Ardo's left. The horrendous creature turned suddenly to face the light, just as Ardo got his bearings. The long, deep-ivory talons extending from each of its forearms snapped toward the terrified Marine. The Zergling's vomit-brown head cowl reared back as it screeched hideously.

Ardo had no time to think. Training. Instinct. He swiveled the weapon around as the display in his helmet switched automatically to attack mode.

The Zergling lunged down the corridor, its massive hind legs with razor-spine edges propelling it at incredible speed directly toward the Marine.

"*Thou shalt not kill,*" the voice whispered unheeded at the back of his mind.

Ardo pulled the trigger, leaning into the rifle as he did.

Steel-tipped infantry slugs tore from the muzzle of the gauss automatic rifle at thirty rounds per second. Fifteen sonic booms rattled in the air.

Ardo released the trigger. Short bursts. Training.

Fully half the initial burst had found its mark, ripping through the flesh of the Zergling, splattering the walls with the detritus. Greenish-black ichor poured from the gaping holes punched in the creature's torso.

The Zergling did not slow.

Ten meters separated them now.

Ardo pulled the trigger once more. *Longer bursts,* he thought automatically, his conscious, screaming mind pushed aside.

The gauss rifle chattered again, the tracers registering in Ardo's facial display, correcting his aim at the juggernaut of death and hatred clawing toward him. Pieces of the creature's carapace broke away, slamming against the walls and clattering to the hard floor of the spore tunnel. Black blood spurted from the exposed arteries as the creature shook with each impact.

Ardo released again.

Five meters.

The Zergling, frothing from its fanged mouth, reeled with the impacts but—impossibly—found its feet and lunged forward.

Ardo, eyes wide with terror, jammed down on the trigger. The gauss rifle responded almost instantly, sending a stream of hot metal against and through his enemy. Still it pressed toward him against the steel-tipped hail slamming through it. Ardo's training evaporated in that instant. A scream, raw and unconscious in its intensity, erupted from his throat. The animal within him took hold. The Confederacy ceased to exist. The Marines ceased to exist. There was just Ardo, his back against the wall, fighting for his life.

One meter.

Ardo's eyes were fixed open, unblinking, as the hideous, alien face loomed closer still.

The gauss rifle stopped chattering despite Ardo's fanatical grip on the trigger. The magazine was empty.

The smooth, mottled brown of the Zergling face smashed against Ardo's faceplate. Ardo could not look away. He peered into the black, soul-less eyes just inches from his face. His hands mindlessly shook the assault rifle, hoping against reason that it would somehow, impossibly, start up again.

Ardo could not stop screaming.

Slowly, the face of the Zergling slid down the faceplate, its torso bumping against Ardo's arms.

Ardo scrambled backward, the boots of his battle-suit slipping slightly as he kicked himself back away from the shattered remains of the revolting creature. Ardo shakily ejected the magazine from the assault rifle. He banged the new magazine against his head to clear any sand, more out of instinct than any real need, before he slammed it home in the rifle and primed the weapon once more.

The Zergling lay at his feet. Nearly half of the carapace had been shot away. Ardo could see one of its arms had been severed and blown back to rest on the ground farther down the spore corridor. A widening pool of black was spreading across the corridor floor beneath it.

It still breathed.

"All creatures of our God and King," his mother sang. *"Lift up your voice and hear us sing . . ."*

Ardo began to shake uncontrollably.

He was twelve in Sunday school class. "But these, as natural brute beasts, made to be taken and destroyed, speak evil of the things that they understand not; and shall utterly perish in their own corruption . . ." Beasts were interesting to a twelve-year-old. . . .

The Zergling twitched before him. The beast's dull, black eye stared back at him.

"And God said, Let the waters bring forth abundantly the moving creature that hath life . . ."

Ardo could not breathe.

Panicked, he suddenly dropped his rifle. His hands clawed at the faceplate release. It resisted for a moment, and then slid sideways with a definitive click. He slammed the visor open as he fell down on all fours.

His breakfast gushed in a cascade against the floor of the spore tunnel. His arms supported him but continued to shake uncontrollably. Again, he heaved; then again.

It was not until then that he noticed the stench in the shaft other than his own. He belched twice and knew he was dry. He wiped his hand on his now-soiled battle armor before he reached up and snapped the visor shut against the smell.

Finally, spent and weak, he tried to push himself back up. He found that he could not stand. So he sat with his back against the wall of the shaft and drew his armored knees up to his chest.

"Thou shalt not kill . . ."

The Zergling stopped twitching. He watched it die in front of him and wondered how he could have taken a life—life that only God could grant.

Ardo had killed.

"Thou shalt not kill. . . ."

The Marine began to weep quietly, rocking back and forth as he squatted at the bottom of the shaft.

He had killed. He had never killed before. He had been trained, conditioned, drilled, and simulated more ways and times than he could ever recall. But until this moment, he had never truly deprived anything of its life.

His mother had taught him it was a sin to kill. His father had taught him to respect all life, as life was a gift from God. Where were his parents now? Where was their faith now? Where was their hope? Dead with them on a distant world called Bountiful. Destroyed by these same mindless demons from hell, he told himself. Yet the words sounded hollow to him, excuses for the truth, as his father used to say to him.

". . . and every living creature that moveth, which the

waters brought forth abundantly, after their kind, and every winged fowl after his kind: and God saw that it was good."

Ardo drew his knees up tighter. He could not seem to think.

The display on the inside of his visor began to flash insistently. The motion sensors had picked up activity in the blackness of the spore tunnel that stretched before him, but Ardo's mind seemed frozen, unable to grasp its importance.

"I'm sorry, Mom," Ardo mumbled through his tears. "I didn't mean to do it. I didn't mean to . . ."

The headset began to crackle in his ears.

"An eye for an eye . . . a tooth for a tooth . . ."

Ardo hugged his knees tighter.

". . . down . . . Sarge! . . . this hole!" The crackling began to form words. Ardo barely heard them, as if they were from a conversation a great distance away.

The faceplate display locked onto the motion. The readout began updating: sixty meters and closing.

". . . this shaft." Suddenly the sound came clear into Ardo's ears. He vaguely recognized the voice as Bernelli's. "*Shit!* Must be a hundred feet down. Hey, Melnikov! You still . . ."

Ardo blinked and took a shuddering breath.

Multiple contacts appeared on his visor display. Their number was steadily increasing.

". . . down an old well shaft, Sarge," the voice continued to crackle in his ears. "The creep must have covered it over and he fell through. I think I can see him but he ain't answerin' me."

Forty meters and closing.

Mom was gone. Dad was gone. Melani was gone. *I'm the only one left to remember them,* Ardo realized.

Thirty-five meters and closing.

He looked up. He could see the lights from Bernelli's suit flashing in the distance above.

Someone has to live.

"I'm here," he called up as he reached quickly down and retrieved his gauss rifle from the debris-covered floor. He quickly pulled the grapple from his belt and slid it down the muzzle of the rifle. "Stand back; grapple's coming up."

"Hey, man, we thought we'd lost you!"

"Not today," he called back.

Thirty meters and closing.

He fired the grapple straight up the shaft. The monofilament line whipped upward, spooling out from the automated winch in the back of his power armor.

He looked back down the shaft just as he activated the lift. A cold smile formed on his tear-streaked face as his feet quickly cleared the floor of the spore tunnel.

"Not today."

CHAPTER 7

SPIT AND POLISH

CUTTER'S ENORMOUS FISTS REACHED DOWN AND dragged Ardo up out of the hole, combat armor and all. He had barely cleared the lip of the cave-in before three of his squad began firing down into the hole he had just vacated.

"Sarge!" Alley cried out, a little more excitement in his voice than he would have liked. "They're coming up. *Shit!* There's no end to 'em!"

"Don't just stand there, *damn it!* Fire at will!" Littlefield shouted through the command channel.

"Hoggin' it all, were you, punk?" the islander growled through his faceplate pressed against Ardo's own. "Thought you might just be the hero of the hour takin' 'em on all by yourself?"

"Back off, Cutter," Littlefield said sharply. "The lieutenant wants a word with this kid right now. Alley! You keep up the suppressing fire. Ekart, Xiang, start fragging this hole right now! Bernelli, you set a charge. When you've finished with them, I don't want the Zerg even *thinking* of putting a hole here again! Soon as you can, get your butts over to the Admin Office. Keep an eye out. If there's one spore hole there's bound to be more and I don't want any of them tappin' me on the shoulder. Clear?"

The squad nodded their consent as they rained death down the hole at their feet.

"Cutter, keep an eye on these whelps and get them back to me in one piece."

"Damn it, Sarge!" Cutter protested. "I haven't killed a thing all day!"

Littlefield seemed to consider the Firebat Marine for a moment. There was sadness in his eyes but his voice was solid and clear. "You'll have plenty lined up for you before the day's out, Cutter. I'll need those men. Get them back to me, clear?"

"Clear, sir," Cutter sniffed. "Glass-clear."

Littlefield turned to Ardo. "On the quick, Marine! Let's go!"

Sergeant Littlefield wasted no time and had bounded several steps ahead of Ardo before the younger Marine caught on. Littlefield ran through the alleys of Oasis while Ardo tried desperately to keep up. The creep was still underfoot. Ardo expected at any moment to crash once more through the brittle crust and tumble into a worse situation than before. Much as he feared that, there was something deep inside him that feared disobeying the sergeant's orders even more.

The tactical channel did not give him a clear picture of what was going on, but what he understood did not sound good.

"Holy shit, man! They're not stoppin'!"

"Keep fraggin' 'em, man!"

"I am, man! I'm nearly out . . ."

"Stand back, you ladies! Time to light me some Zerg!"

Cutter, Ardo thought as he ducked down another alley, trying desperately to keep up with Littlefield.

Oasis had been a small outpost. There was little to offer here other than the work, which the wells and multiple pumping stations provided. Homes were largely of the modular variety, each showing the very temporary nature of their construction. The central district of the settlement had a small number of shops, which served the locals.

At least, they *used* to serve the locals. The creep had extended itself down the length of the central section of the town. *There must be a bloom around here somewhere*, Ardo thought, but he was having trouble keeping up with Littlefield through the maze of haphazardly placed buildings and had little time to think about it.

". . . it's shifting, Sergeant! The creep is starting to move!"

"Well, find the bloom. We find that and we can take it all out."

"I've been looking. It just ain't here."

"We'll make a high pass over the main street again. Maybe we missed it."

The four Vulture hover-cycles screamed overhead

just as the central administration building came into view. It was not difficult to find. Three stories high, it towered over all the other occupied buildings in the settlement. A gaping, ragged hole had been torn in one side of the building, its external metal wall peeled back; whether by an explosion or some unthinkably powerful hands, Ardo did not care to speculate.

He was so astonished at the sight that he nearly ran directly into Sergeant Littlefield, who had stopped abruptly short of the admin building. The older man looked into the eyes of the panting Ardo, who now stood confused before him, and then keyed his transmitter to Squad Member Select. His words were for Ardo alone.

"Son, you're in a lot of trouble, but don't sweat it. Just take it like a Marine and I think things are going to be okay. Understand?"

Ardo nodded even though he knew it was a lie. He was having trouble understanding much of anything at the moment. "Sir, yes, sir!"

Littlefield smiled. "Well, there isn't much they can do to you out here that the job won't do for them. Be polite, don't talk back to Breanne, and I think you may just live to rejoin my squad. She's waiting for you up in Operations."

Littlefield gave Ardo's battle armor a quick glance, then smiled. "I wish we had time to hose you off first, son! You're gonna smell just awful for the lieutenant."

*   *   *

You would have thought they would have at least removed the dead, Ardo thought, as he stepped into the Operations Room.

Operations was at the top of the three-story central building in the complex. Its windows, now vacant of all but the smallest shards of glass, looked out over the settlement. The building had probably been the last stand of the colonists, and when the fight was over there was nobody left to bury the dead.

That had been several days ago. The Confederacy Marines had given the Zerg a pretty good pasting when they reached Scenic. Intel called it an "extermination" and believed that only a minimal force of Zerg remained in Oasis. Still, no one in command had thought it necessary to come back to the pumping settlement and honor the valiant fallen. After all, they *were* dead.

The Operations Room itself had seen considerable damage. Several Marines from Second Squad were working to shore up the gaping holes in the outer wall. The sporadic light from their hand welders played a ghastly blue-white pall across the grizzly scene. In the center of the room, the lieutenant leaned over the map table, her back toward them. Her battle armor helmet was off, sitting to one side as she tried to concentrate on the readout in front of her.

Ardo could still hear her on the tactical channel.

"Third Squad continue north toward the tower and then fall back toward Operations."

"I've got movement over here! Something's coming!"

"Shut up, man! We've all got movement . . . everywhere! They're coming out of the floor, man!"

"Keep moving! Keep moving!"

Sergeant Littlefield unlatched his helmet and quickly tucked it into the crook of his left arm. "Beggin' your pardon, ma'am? Reporting as ordered."

The lieutenant straightened and began to turn.

Ardo barely had the presence of mind to quickly remove his own helmet and salute.

The smell in the room was more familiar than what he had experienced in the spore tunnel, and therefore all the more nauseating.

Her voice was coated in frost. "Private . . . Melnikov, isn't it? How good of you to obey an order at last." Her eyes flicked over toward the sergeant. "Mr. Littlefield, do you think this fresh-out-of-the-can Marine is worth my trouble?"

"Ma'am . . . by your grace, ma'am!" Ardo glanced sideways at the sergeant. There seemed to be a smile playing at the edge of his mouth.

"I doubt it," Breanne snapped. "Step forward, Private!"

Ardo panicked. He was saluting and could not move until the salute had been returned, yet he had just been ordered to move. Something in his brain seized up, and he seemed unable to do much of anything except sweat and continue to hold his salute.

Breanne seemed suddenly to understand this. She

swore under her breath and offered a perfunctory salute.

Relieved, Ardo dropped the salute, and shuddered slightly as he stepped over a headless torso and arm. He could not tell if it had been a man or a woman. He did not want to know. He kept his eyes fixed on the lieutenant.

"Mister Melnikov! Did I or did I not order this team to hold weapons fire for this operation?"

It was a direct question. Ardo could not help but give an answer. "Ma'am! Yes, ma'am!"

"Did I not make it clear that this was a recon and extraction mission?"

"Ma'am! Glass-clear, ma'am!"

Breanne's face was getting uncomfortably close to Ardo's own. Her words were chilling. "Then why, soldier, did you disobey my order?"

Ardo swallowed. "Fell down a shaft, ma'am! Encountered a Zerg . . ." He stammered slightly, the memory of it flooding over him all at once. He dropped his eyes, suddenly ashamed. "I . . . I killed it!"

"Look at me when I'm talking to you, soldier!"

Ardo's eyes locked on her sharp nose.

"You think that's what we're here for, to kill Zerg?"

"Ma'am! Yes, ma'am! Send them all to hell, ma'am!"

Breanne rolled her eyes at this and stepped away, seething. "Littlefield, can you believe this? *This* is the new Marine! Neural resocialization! Cookie-cutter soldiers! Press them out of the resoc tanks like so many gingerbread men, wind 'em up and send 'em off to die!"

Littlefield chuckled darkly. "Well, ma'am, it's a lot quicker than the old way, that's for sure. That's progress."

"God save us from progress!" Breanne sighed, then turned her steel eyes back on Ardo. "Mr. Melnikov, let me try to educate you the old-fashioned way. Private, we are *not* here to kill Zerg."

Ardo felt confused. "Ma'am?"

"We are here to *stop* Zerg. That's a different thing altogether. Those caseless steel-tipped infantry rounds you so dutifully loaded into your assault rifle this morning are not designed to kill. They are designed to maim."

"Ma'am, I . . . I don't understand."

"Kill a man on the field of battle and you can leave him there. The buzzards will take care of him." Breanne gestured around the Operations Room. "Look around you, Private. There was nothing we could do for the dead. You honor them when you can, but in the middle of battle there's nothing you can do for them. They are *no longer of any concern*, understand?"

"Well . . . yes, ma'am, but . . ."

"But nothing! If you *maim* an enemy on the field it takes four of his friends to haul him back from the battle and even *more* of his friends to patch him up and care for him. Kill an enemy and you decrease the force against you by one. *Maim* an enemy and you decrease the force against you by *ten*. Is any of this sinking in through that thick, resocialized brain of yours?"

Ardo thought for a moment. "Yes, ma'am."

"Then perhaps in the future you will be more careful in the field to follow my orders *to the letter*?"

"Ma'am, yes, ma'am . . . but . . ."

Breanne's eyes narrowed. "Are you trying to say something, Private?"

Ardo swallowed. "Begging your pardon, ma'am . . . but is the lieutenant suggesting that it would have been better for me to have died at the bottom of that well?"

Breanne took a breath to answer, then held it in check. A wicked smile rippled across her lips. "Well, well, well! A Marine who thinks! How refreshing. There's hope for you yet, Melnikov. I—"

"Hey, Lieutenant! I think we found something!"

"Marz, here. They've got something on one of the scanners."

"Hey, I think I found it!"

Breanne spun back toward the map table. "Where? Where is it?"

"It's just a prefab house . . . I think it's in a basement."

"Lordy! The ground is breaking all around me!"

"Movement! Movement!"

"Where?"

"Everywhere!"

"Cutter!" Breanne snapped. "Get the device! Marz! They're at . . . damn it! . . . map grid thirty-six mark four-seventeen. Get them out of there!"

"They'll be vulnerable if I do, Lieutenant! Get them back to Operations and I'll pick up the lot of ya."

"Captain Marz, get that crate over there and pick up my team!"

"There's no place to set down, Lieutenant, and if I use the extraction fields they'll be held in stasis on the ground for a few seconds. That's more than enough time for the Zerg to kill them where they stand."

"That's just great!"

Breanne motioned for Littlefield to join her. The sergeant quickly stepped up to the map table. He began pointing to various locations as Breanne spoke.

"Second Squad, get that device. First Squad, I need high cover for Second Squad at thirty-six mark four-seventeen!"

"Hey, does she mean us, man?"

"You heard the lady, it's just over— Sweet shit! Where did they come from?"

"It's a whole goddamn wall of 'em!"

"More like a carpet! Where the hell did they come from?"

"Third Squad!" Breanne continued. "Cover fire from thirty-four mark four-sixteen to thirty-six mark four-sixteen. Hold a corridor open and then fall back."

"Say again?"

"I said, hold a corridor and then fall back with Second Squad to the operations center. We'll extract from here."

The lieutenant turned to Ardo.

"Well, you started this, Melnikov, now you can help clean it up. Join Third Squad and see if you can get your old Second Squad back here in as few pieces as possible."

The lieutenant turned back to the map.

"I think it is safe to say that they know we are here now."

CHAPTER 8

SEEING THE ELEPHANT

ARDO DASHED DOWN THE STAIRWELL, STEPPING quickly over the bodies along the way, then burst into what once was the lobby. Wabowski, the second Fire-bat in the platoon, was already charging up his plasma flamethrower. Mellish and Esson were both fingering their gauss rifles nervously. Sejak seemed even more agitated than the others.

"Where's Jensen?" Ardo asked.

"Went to find M'butu," Sejak said, licking his lips. "He said he'd only be . . . oh, *hell*, he's overdue."

"I say we go find him," Wabowski rumbled.

"And I say we follow orders," Littlefield snapped, coming down the stairs and joining them. "The lieutenant knows what she's doing. You've got the word and you know the drill. Move it, people! On me!"

Littlefield readied his own assault rifle and moved out through the broken doors of the lobby. The broken squad glanced around at each other for a moment and then moved quickly to follow the sergeant.

The wind was blowing a steady, hot breeze from the northeast, kicking dust up over the creep that had spread across the main square. Ardo shuddered as they moved across it. They could all hear Cutter and the rest of First and Second squads on the command channel, disembodied voices struggling to survive somewhere beyond the wall of buildings surrounding the outpost's central square.

"Keep moving! Keep moving!"

"Bowers? Bowers! Where the hell . . ."

"Bowers is down!"

"Fu! Peaches! Get your asses over here, now!"

"Damn! Sarge! I'm hit! I'm hit! The cycle's dropping down! Help me! Oh, God . . . they're gonna be all over me! Don't let them . . ."

Littlefield's voice echoed in their helmets, his proximity automatically overriding the other voices, fading them below his own. "Sejak! Mellish! You two take flanking positions on the square and hold it. Wabowski, you and the rest of the squad come with me on point. I don't want anything comin' up behind me, Marines!"

Ardo followed without a word, though he was shaking inside his battle armor. The private glanced to either side nervously as he moved forward purely out of training. Somewhere in the back of his mind was the instinct to run in the other direction as quickly as his battle armor would take him, but the training kept that howling animal somehow at bay.

"Alley! Get the hell out of my way! I'll burn 'em!"

"They're a frickin' wall, Cutter!"

"Keep moving! Hang onto that box, Ekart, or I swear to God I'll make you go back for it, Zerg or no! Keep moving!"

Wabowski was on Ardo's left, laden down with two fully charged plasma tanks mounted into the back of his Firebat flamethrower battle armor. Esson flanked Wabowski on the far side. Though Ardo could not see him directly, his helmet display noted M'butu directly behind them. They were in the classic support position for Firebats, something Ardo gave no more thought to than the others following Littlefield across the square. One might as well concentrate on thinking about how to breathe. Everything and everyone was performing by the book.

Then why, Ardo thought, *am I still shaking?*

"Hell! They're everywhere! Where are they comin' from?"

"Keep movin', grunt!"

They reached a barricade on the far side of the square that extended across the eastern road between two buildings. It had obviously been thrown together from whatever was at hand. Two heavy loaders and a mobile trencher formed the bulk of the barricade, but anything within reach appeared to have been pressed into service. Desks, beds, rocks, pieces of broken wall, even a pair of children's cycles had been tossed desperately onto the pile. From the look of the mangled dead who remained, their efforts may have bought them an extra minute and a half.

Ardo shook violently, suddenly dreadfully afraid

that his teeth would chatter over the com frequency. He concentrated on what the lieutenant had said. *"There's nothing you can do for them. They are no longer of any concern, understand?"* Still, Ardo looked away, feeling vaguely ashamed.

Littlefield took no notice of Ardo's discomfort. He scanned the eastern road that wound between the buildings. Calling it a road was generous; it was more of a tortured passage that ran crookedly between modular buildings. "There they are," the sergeant said, pointing eastward.

Ardo peered between the buildings. Something was moving beyond the fine veil of blowing red dust, but he could not be sure just what. The wind was picking up with the evening, the blowing dust obscuring his vision even more. The chatter from the com channel was getting louder and more distinct. Cutter was making progress, but would it be enough?

"M'butu! Esson!" Littlefield's words were level and matter-of-fact. Just another day at the office, he seemed to be saying. "You anchor both sides of this barricade. Set up a crossfire down this passage. Melnikov!"

Ardo looked to the sergeant at the sound of his name.

"You and Wabowski come with me. Let's bring 'em in."

With that, Littlefield leveled his gauss rifle and clambered over the barricade.

Ardo could not move.

Littlefield was already getting hard to see, the blowing dust fading the sergeant's battle armor in and out.

Ardo's mind seemed to seize up. He could not move forward. He could not move back.

Suddenly, something slammed against the middle of his back, knocking him forward.

"Come on, Melnikov," Wabowski sniffed. "Move your ass! This is a rescue mission, remember?"

Wabowski's booted foot dislodged Ardo's stupor. They both scrambled over the barricade quickly, Ardo covering both the barely discernible Littlefield and Wabowski behind him.

"Left!" Wabowski yelled suddenly.

Ardo spun, crouching.

Several Zerg were clawing their way with incredible speed along the wall of a modular building. They seemed to defy gravity through raw strength. The moment Ardo recognized them, the first of them leaped from the wall, directly toward the Marine.

Ardo had no time to think. He squeezed the trigger of the gauss assault rifle. The hail of slugs smashed into the monster midair. The raw strength of the creature might have impelled it forward, but the accelerated projectiles arrested the Zerg's momentum and pinned it against the wall. The remaining creatures crouched down against the wall, preparing to spring on their own.

A sudden column of plasma flame engulfed the

wall, swallowing the Zerg in its fury. Ardo turned around and saw Wabowski, a huge grin on his face, hosing the wall down with the plasma stream.

He also saw the Zerg lurkers cresting the top of the building behind the smiling Firebat warrior.

"On your back!" Ardo yelled, his voice sounding high-pitched in his own ears. His rifle chattered in his hands, laying down a pattern across the rooftop. Several of the lurkers dropped heavily to the ground, their claws working in the dust, struggling to bring them closer to their prey.

We are the prey, Ardo suddenly realized. He could see the smile on Wabowski's face had suddenly waxed grim. The bursts of superheated plasma were flashing toward several targets at Ardo's own back.

"Keep 'em off me, brother," Wabowski drawled. "I'm a little busy here."

The slick, dark forms suddenly seemed to be everywhere on the modules lining the street. Ardo remembered as a child once kicking an anthill on his father's farm, and the ants appeared as if by magic to be all around him at once.

I kicked this anthill, Ardo thought.

The rifle suddenly stopped chattering. Instinctively, Ardo ejected the clip, banged a new clip against his helmet, and slammed it home into the rifle. The clip had barely reached the breach when Ardo pulled the trigger again, splaying the advancing and ever increasing hordes of Zerg lurkers dropping down like rain from the southern rooftops.

"Damn! How far do we have to go?"

"We'll never make it, Cutter!"

"Shut up! Keep moving!"

"We are under heavy attack!" Wabowski's words were factual, but there was a definite edge to them. "Littlefield, if you're going to do something, now would be the time!"

"Got 'em, Wabowski. ETA your position one minute."

Ardo's second clip emptied. Sweat streaming down his face despite the climate control of the battle armor, he ejected the clip once more and pressed the third clip home even as he squeezed the trigger. The broken, mutilated bodies of the lurkers were falling on top of each other. The pile itself was drawing closer to him by the minute, scratching the ground, desperate for Ardo's blood.

Still they came over the eaves of the roof. Ardo could only imagine what Wabowski was fighting out of sight behind his own back.

Ardo's gauss rifle was warm in his hands. The suit filtered that sensation so that it would not do him any actual harm, but he knew that it meant the rifle was getting dangerously close to seizing up.

"We got contact." It was Mellish, behind them in the square. *"Fire zone here in the square. We could use some help back here!"*

One of the Zerg claws reached out from the pile, snapping blindly at Ardo's leg. He took an instinctive step back, then sent a quick burst downward that severed the limb entirely.

When he looked up, the rooftop lurkers were already in midair, leaping toward him.

They never reached the ground. A burst of flame and gauss slugs from Ardo's left obliterated them.

"Make way, kid," Cutter said, his huge Firebat suit running past Ardo at full speed. There appeared to be a civilian draped over the huge man's shoulder as he plunged forward. He held the figure in place with one hand and wielded the massive plasma hose with the other. He shouted through the com channel as he ran. "Keep moving!"

Littlefield and Xiang rushed past as well, holding a metallic case by its handles between them. Bernelli continued to fire his own rifle, sometimes at real targets and sometimes at imaginary ones.

"Stay and hold 'em, Melnikov!" Littlefield shouted as he passed. The case appeared to be heavy, slowing Xiang and him down. "We're almost there! Wabowski! Buy us time! That's an order!"

Ardo turned to look east down the road.

Zerg poured down the street, their talons a wall of death and hatred. Ardo knew that they had come for him. Wildly, he thought that they knew, somehow, that he had escaped them twice before. They wanted him, his flesh, his blood.

Ardo turned and ran.

Wabowski continued to rake the walls with the plasma stream, unaware that Ardo had left him.

The lurkers on the opposite wall leaped.

Ardo turned at the scream. The Zerg lurkers had

ripped the nozzle from Wabowski's hands and were savagely raking the armor, prying at it carefully. They apparently knew better than to tear haphazardly into a Firebat suit. They would take it apart in moments, dragging the screaming Wabowski out and then . . .

Three Hydralisks grasped Melani at once, dragging her back from the edge of the crowd.

"Please, Ardo," she wept. *"Don't leave me alone!"*

Ardo raised his weapon and fired a stream of armor-piercing rounds into the tanks of Wabowski's Firebat suit.

Firebat suits are dangerous even under the best of conditions. The containment fields shattered, Wabowski erupted into a mammoth conflagration, a roiling ball that engulfed the buildings around it, swallowing the Zerg, who were too intent on their prey. The flames rolled between the buildings, an expanding inferno raging down the channel directly toward Ardo.

CHAPTER 9

FALL BACK

"MELNIKOV!"

Ardo turned at the sound of his name crackling in his helmet.

"Move it, Marine! *Damn it,* Melnikov! Answer me!"

The fireball roiled behind him, eating the air between the buildings. He sensed its hunger and its power at his back. He began to run toward the barricade at the end of the crooked street, already brilliantly lit by the approaching flames.

Ardo's feet were like lead. His arms and legs moved in agonizing slowness. Time was working against him. He tried to cry out for help, but the words seemed malformed and incoherent in his own ears.

The brightness suddenly enveloped him. Chaos erupted in his helmet. Half a dozen different alarms rang out, but he had no time to pay attention to any of them. He was swimming through the brilliant flame and heat. The suit servos strained against the explosive force, struggling to keep Ardo's various limbs and appendages where they belonged. He tumbled through the fire, the heat overcoming the internal cooling. Ardo could feel the webflex netting of the undersuit searing his flesh. All sense of up or down, in or out, was lost as panic welled up within him.

Suddenly he fell from the sky. The ground rushed up at him, slamming his head violently against the interior of his helmet. Dazed, he felt as though he were still moving, although the rough granules of dirt and rock half burying his faceplate belied the thought. He lay still for a moment, aware of a thin stream of blood winding its way down across the clear plexithene of the faceplate and slowly starting to pool.

He jerked himself upright, the movement smearing his blood across both the inside of his helmet and his face. Littlefield was crabbing backward next to him, dragging the ungainly metal case. Xiang had been helping him with it just moments before. Ardo vaguely wondered what had happened to him. The sergeant's gauss rifle was chattering in his hands, spitting out a stream of death. Other members of the squad were backing away from the barricade as well.

"Keep moving! Keep moving!" Littlefield yelled, though they all could have heard him perfectly well through the com-system.

Ardo staggered unsteadily to his feet. Next to him, the sergeant turned suddenly on his heel, his weapon instinctively training on the movement so close to his side. Fear and desperation registered for a moment on the old veteran's features. Ardo half expected to be cut down where he so unsteadily stood, but the sergeant's trigger finger held back long enough for him to register who was suddenly in his sights.

"*Goddamn*, Melnikov! You're a hard man to kill!" Littlefield said, with a hint of hysterical laughter in his voice. Littlefield turned back to face the barricade. "Fall back! Listen to me! Fall back *now!*"

The inferno from Wabowski's explosion continued to rage enthusiastically down the length of the street beyond the barricade, preventing most of the Zerg groundlings from reaching them. Here and there, however, pockets of them somehow managed to swarm through the flames. Cutter, his huge Firebat armor towering over the remaining members of the detail, was still pumping short bursts of plasma against the Zerg as they tried repeatedly to swarm over the barricade. Ardo gaped. Cutter was firing his plasma weapon with a single hand while still holding on with his other hand to the rag-doll survivor slung over his shoulder.

"It's working," Ardo whispered, more to himself than to the sergeant standing next to him. "We're holding them off."

"Like *hell* we are," Littlefield snapped. "They're cunning, these slime-bugs. They'll keep us occupied here with a few of their kin just long enough to circle around and take us from behind. Make yourself useful, Melnikov, and grab the other side of this case!" The sergeant turned his attention once more to the hulking Firebat. "Cutter, get that civilian out of here!

Sejak! Ekart! Lay down cover fire and pull back to oh-thirty-seven mark one-fifty-three. We got our little prize, now let's get the hell out of here!"

Cutter growled through the com-system, but he obeyed, falling back with the rest of the line. The shining carapaces of the Zerglings leaped deftly over the barricades with a grace and speed Ardo had not thought possible. Each in turn was met by concentrated fire from the retreating Marines.

"How we doin', boss?" Littlefield called out.

"*Clock's running out.*" It was the lieutenant, still in the Operations tower that somehow in Ardo's mind was suddenly miles away. "*I can't see them on tactical, but you know they've got to be coming for us. I'm abandoning the Ops center now. Double-time to oh-thirty-seven mark one-fifty-three. We'll dust off there. You copy that, Peaches?*"

"*Yes, ma'am.*" The voice had a strange edge to it. If Peaches was answering on the command channel, then things had not gone well for the Vulture cycle crews.

"Vixen, *you got the coordinates?*"

"*You just get your pretty ass over there, and the* Vixen *will do the rest. Pick up and delivery! ETA five minutes to dust off.*"

"Let's go, people!" Littlefield rumbled. "We don't have a lot of time!"

Cutter growled through the com-system and then turned. One glance and Ardo could see the look on the man's face. His words were for Littlefield, but his cold, black eyes were trained squarely on Ardo as he spoke. "Beg to report one Firebat lost, sir! Wabowski, sir!"

Ardo quickly snatched at the handle on the metal box. His armor was power enhanced, but the feedback systems let him know that it was heavy.

"Let's move," Littlefield snapped.

In tandem, the two of them began running back across the square. Littlefield pointed off to the left of the Operations tower. Ardo sensed the rest of the squad falling back with them, collapsing the perimeter as they dashed toward the extraction point.

Ardo ran, but he could not clear his mind. "Sergeant . . . sir, about Wabowski, I . . ."

"That was one *hell* of a move, kid," Littlefield cut in, the box bouncing erratically between them as they ran. "Wabowski was already a dead man. You did him a favor . . . and we are wasting what little time you bought for us."

"Yeah . . . thanks." Cutter was running just behind them. The helmet obstructed Ardo's view of the huge islander, but he knew from the big man's tone that he was anything but appreciative.

"You just keep hold of that civilian, Cutter, and leave the thinking to me. As for you, Melnikov . . . if you're still alive by the end of the day"—Littlefield huffed between quick breaths—"well then, by God, son, you may be a veteran yet!"

Cutter's voice was all venom just two steps behind him. "A veteran, eh, Melnikov? Oh, then by all means, you go first. I've seen what you can do with a rifle, and I think it's better if I *follow* you."

"*ETA two minutes. Vixen turning downwind now. Jeez! Look at 'em down there! You really stirred up the hive, didn't you, Breanne!*"

They ran down the line of buildings, checking their flanks as they went. There was definitely something out there, but nothing Ardo could really see. Dark movement flashed in the gaps between structures. *Don't stop to look,* he told himself, the rhythm of his running steps in counterpoint. *Don't stop or they'll take you down.*

"*Hold fire! Hold fire at oh-thirty-five!*" It was Breanne's voice. Ardo glanced toward the navigation radial. Sure enough, the lieutenant was running toward them, her own rifle held at the ready. There were three soldiers running with her, two less than he had seen her with only fifteen minutes before.

"Don't stop! Keep moving!" The lieutenant did not break stride as she urged them forward. "Is that the prize, Littlefield?"

"Yes, ma'am!" Littlefield picked up his pace a little to keep up with Breanne. Ardo, still clinging to the other side of the metal case, was forced to do the same.

"Nice work, Sergeant!" Lieutenant Breanne was looking toward the rapidly approaching opening at the end of the street. "So, who is the meat that Cutter is hauling out of here?"

"Don't know, ma'am. Some civvy he found still breathing when they came across the box."

"Well, Cutter, looks like you've rescued yourself a real live princess." A smile played into Breanne's voice. "Hang onto her, Private. I'll want to talk with her once we get out of this."

Ardo could hear the filtered chatter of gauss rifle fire over his intercom. Someone nearby was firing short bursts.

"Contact, Lieutenant!" It was Mellish. "On the right!"

"I see 'em, too!" Bernelli was running picket for the retreat on the left. "*Damn! Look at 'em move!*"

Breanne looked up as she ran. "*Vixen!* What's your status?"

"*Turning base now. Keep your skirt on, Lieutenant, I'll be there in . . . oh, hell! Stand by.*"

The squad burst from the shelter of the surrounding buildings. The supply-landing pad for Oasis stretched out all around them. Several battered hangars and warehouses stood to either side. After the claustrophobic trails between the buildings, the area felt exposed and vulnerable. Beyond the landing pad toward the south was an open expanse of hydrofarms and the long road they had followed earlier in the day to reach Oasis. Ardo could see the vertical cliff wall of the Basin in the distant south. Molly's Nipple was hazy in the distance, and he could make out the Stonewall Peaks. Right between them, he knew, lay Scenic and their fortified base.

It seemed a million miles away.

Private William Peaches and Private Amy Windom

were landing their Vulture cycles in the center of the open area. When the day began, the Vultures had numbered five. Now they were down to two.

"Littlefield! Melnikov!" The lieutenant moved toward the parked Vultures at the center of the landing pad. "Keep that box near me! Cutter! Bring that civvy, too. Everyone else, I need an extraction perimeter around me *now!*"

Ardo could see the windsock next to the landing field. He kept glancing to the south and the distant ridges where a clean bunk, a shower, and, perhaps, relative safety might be found. He had killed twice in one day. He longed for unconsciousness. If Captain Marz was following a standard approach, he should be coming from that direction.

Breanne was looking in the same direction, searching the sky for any sign of movement.

"*Vixen,*" she called out. "Update!"

The Confederacy Marines formed a circle on the landing pad, training their weapons outward. The sands of the Basin were blowing across the flat expanse, obscuring the once carefully laid-out markings. Ardo could hear the swish of the sand blowing against the hard carapace of his own battle armor.

Nothing else.

"*Vixen.*" Breanne's voice was steady. "We are on station. What is your ETA?"

The com channel crackled with muffled background static, the gain automatically heightening as the equipment strained to hear a response.

"Lieutenant! We've got movement!"

"Where, Bernelli?"

"Just past the hangars, ma'am! They're flanking us on the east just beyond—"

"West, too, Lieutenant! Gods! Look at how *fast* they are!"

"*Vixen!* Damn it! Report!" Breanne turned back to the south. "Littlefield! Do you see him? He said he was a minute inbound. We should have seen him by now."

"He should have been here by now, Lieutenant," Littlefield replied. "There's something wrong here, ma'am."

Breanne looked south again. "*Vixen!* Come in, *Vixen!* What's your status?"

"He's not there," Littlefield's voice was heavy as he pointed to the south. "But I do see something, ma'am."

Dark figures began moving across the southern end of the landing pad.

"Zerg," Breanne breathed. "They're cutting us off."

Littlefield shook his head. "Lieutenant, I think—"

"They don't pay you to think, Sergeant!" Breanne snapped. "Peaches and Windom! Mount up! Everybody, I want new loads prepped and locked right now! When I give the order, the Vulture cycles open up with everything you have and fly straight across the Zerg line to the south. Plow me a road through those bugs. The rest of us, lead with everything you've got, charge through the hole and don't stop.

Go right through and don't stop for anything, you understand?"

"Then what, Lieutenant?" Esson's voice was a little shaky.

"Then run, boy. Run for the base, and don't look back."

CHAPTER 10

THE GAUNTLET

"THEY'RE CLOSING THE GAP, MA'AM!" BERNELLI whispered hoarsely. It was as though louder noise would somehow shatter a fragile moment and bring the slowly approaching Zerg crashing down on them.

Breanne's voice was cold and level. "Hold your fire, damn it!"

"They're cutting us off, Lieutenant!"

"Shut up, Mellish," Breanne snapped. "Peaches! Can't you get that thing started?"

What remained of the detail was ever so slowly pulling in tighter and tighter around where Ardo stood. The purplish wall of Zerg, their faces locked in a hideous metallic grin, clawed at the air, anxious in anticipation of their prey. Ardo thought suddenly of the cat his mother had barely tolerated to wander about the farm. One afternoon, Ardo had watched in fascinated horror as that otherwise sweet creature had cornered a mouse in the barnyard and played with the trapped prey as though it were a toy. Eventually, that cat had clamped his jaws down on the hapless critter's skull and ended the chase in a bloody, dirty meal. Yet before that happened, Ardo seemed to recall a similar smile on the face of that cat.

And now here he was . . . the mouse.

The Vultures suddenly whined back to life. Ardo could see the sweat breaking out on Peaches as he nervously primed the forward ordnance.

Breanne's voice rose slightly in pitch. Perhaps she was looking at the same teeth as Ardo was considering. "I don't have all day, Priv—"

"I've got it, Lieutenant!" Peaches chattered back. "We're good to go!"

"Very well." Breanne turned slowly, her voice rising over the whine of the Vulture cycles. "Everyone locked and loaded? Peaches and Windom: make me a hole! *now!*"

The Vultures screamed and lurched forward as their riders opened their accelerators clear to the stops. Bolts thundered from their forward projectors and exploded against the Zerg line even as they approached it.

The Zerg screamed, too, their own terrible voices rising in indignation that their prize would have the effrontery to challenge them.

"Now, Marines!" Breanne screamed.

The encroaching outer circle of Zerg suddenly lurched inward, collapsing toward their prey. Their claws whipped through the air, intent on shredding armor, draining blood, and stripping flesh from bones.

Yet the Marines were no longer there. As one they rushed toward the line of explosions before them, the billowing orange conflagration growing by the second. Their weapons trained forward in unison, a solid column of flame and death burning and blasting through the deep column of the enraged Zerg.

"Don't look back! Run, you bastards! Run!"

Ardo ran next to Littlefield, the metal case banging between them. His free hand held his gauss rifle, swinging wildly as it spewed destruction indiscriminately in his path. There was no effort to fire for effect—all he could do as he ran was random damage and add to the carnage already taking place.

They were nearly at the wall of fire they had created. Severed Zerg limbs and burning viscous fluid cascaded around them.

"Keep Firing! Keep running!"

Ardo caught a glimpse of Cutter off to his left. The huge Firebat thundered forward, the female civilian draped over his shoulder. She bounced with each step like a rag doll. With his free hand, Cutter poured plasma into the Zerg line.

The flames wrapped around Ardo as he crossed the line. The footing had already gotten difficult, the ground slick with charred and ruptured Zerg organs. The metal box banged against his leg, letting him know that Littlefield was still there, running and pulling him forward.

An unearthly scream tore across the com channel. It continued, an ear-piercing squeal of terror.

"Esson! *Jeez*, Lieutenant! They're all over him! We gotta—"

"Keep running, Collins! That's an order!"

"But Lieutenant, can't you *hear* him?"

"Run, damn you! Don't look back!"

The internal temperature of Ardo's battle armor was growing by the moment. He could feel his hands and feet starting to blister. Suddenly he ran directly into a standing Zergling. Ardo screamed but did not stop, knocking the creature down in his rush before both vanished from each other's sight amid the conflagration.

He was shocked when, in the next instant, the flame was gone from his smoking faceplate.

Before him lay the long expanse of the southern Basin. Molly's Nipple. The Stonewall Peaks. All he had to do was reach the rim. All he had to do was . . .

The chatter of automatic fire rattled across the com channel.

"They're coming! They're nippin' at my ass! Oh gods of . . ."

A scream drove like a needle into Ardo's ear. Before it died, two more joined it, each unique in its death sound.

"Keep running, you dogs!" Breanne breathed through the com channel. Her own voice had an edge to it Ardo had never heard before. Was she winded or just afraid? "Keep running and don't look back!"

Instinctively, Ardo looked.

The Zerg were closer than he thought and more

numerous than he imagined. To either side of them stretched a carpet of the aliens pouring across the landscape, streaming toward him.

Ardo stumbled at the sight. Littlefield, maintaining a death grip on the case slung between them, shot ahead. Only his companion's pull on the box kept Ardo on his feet and moving forward.

"Do that again, kid," Littlefield huffed between breaths, "and I'll leave you behind."

They were covering open ground now, their battle armor once more carrying them with incredible speed toward the steep incline of the Basin wall. Ardo briefly remembered how much fun he had had crossing this same ground and coming down that incline just a few hours ago. Or was it months ago? In the open, they were widening the distance between themselves and the Zerg behind them. Now he was faced with having to run up that sheer face. Ardo realized with a start that the vertical face would slow down his battle armor considerably, but it would not hinder the enraged Zerg pursuing him.

"Sarge," Ardo huffed. "My weapon's dry. I need to reload."

"Drop it, soldier," Littlefield chuckled with a dry throat.

"Sir?"

"Drop your weapon." Littlefield was a strong warrior, but even his training was being taxed by the full-out run. His words were gasping over his breath. "It doesn't matter anymore, son."

"But, sir!"

"Do you . . . do you know what's . . . what's on top of that cliff right there? There's a bunk and a hot meal waiting . . . for me . . . for you. It's sitting . . . sitting just inside the most beautiful Confederacy per . . . perimeter wall you've ever seen. Auto . . . auto-defense cannon turrets. Bunkers. Prettiest bunkers . . . you've ever seen full . . . full of fresh soldiers who really want to . . . play shooting gallery at a wall of angry Zergs."

Ardo looked at the top of the cliff face again. He could almost see the walls of their base at Scenic. It seemed to be a million steps from where he so desperately continued to run.

"Drop your gun, son," Littlefield croaked. "If we don't clear the rim of this basin . . . no amount of ammo . . . in that fine weapon of yours . . . will save your ass . . . or mine."

Ardo glanced at Littlefield. The old warrior smiled at him through his panting breath. Ardo noticed for the first time that Littlefield had already dropped his weapon and ammunition packs.

Ardo tossed his gun aside, put his head down and ran.

The floor of the basin began to rise in front of them. The relatively smooth floor was giving way to the more uneven terrain leading up to the base of the rim wall. Ardo frantically scrambled across the ever steeper ground, his feet propelling loose rock behind him from time to time. The climb was getting worse with each step. The stone face of the cliff rose above them. The battle armor was powered for many things, but flight was not one of them.

He stumbled onto the access road. It crossed back and forth along the cliff face, a series of switchbacks leading up to Scenic. It was the only way up the cliff.

Ardo risked another glance back. The Marines had put a hundred yards between them and the following Zerg. It would not be enough. The Marines would have to navigate the switchbacks, but Ardo could already see that the Zerg were under no such restraint. The buglike creatures scrambled and leaped over the intervening rocks with barely any check. They would come straight up the cliff face.

Someone else noticed it, too.

"Marines! Prepare to hold and fire!"

Lieutenant Breanne. She was going to stop and make her stand.

"Melnikov. Littlefield. Get that case back to base! Cutter! Follow them with that civilian! That's the mission. The rest of us hold here as long as we can. Maybe it will be enough."

"Holy shit!"

"Shut up, Collins! That line of rocks at the edge of the roadway! Everybody take a position and prepare to fire." Breanne's voice was like steel. She had made up her mind, and nothing and no one could change it now.

The squad, breathless and aching, dashed to the group of protruding boulders lining the side of the road like broken teeth. The Zerg swarm swept toward them.

"Littlefield! Get out of here now or I'll—"

A bright tone sounded suddenly in Ardo's helmet. By the sudden reaction from the remaining platoon members, they all heard it, too.

Ardo, looking at Breanne's face at the time, saw her eyes go wide. She looked up. Ardo followed her gaze and caught a glimpse of a brilliant arching contrail etching itself across the bright sky.

"Turtle down, Marines! Now!" the Lieutenant barked.

Ardo, out of trained reflex more than thought, tossed himself to the ground behind the nearest boulder. He closed his eyes, but to little effect.

The world suddenly went painfully white.

He could feel the concussion through the ground a moment afterward. He had experienced this many times before, but there was still something about being under such primal, unquestioning power that shook him to his soul. It was coming, the great beast, and the shaking ground only heralded its approach.

The shock wave from the tactical nuclear blast had compressed the air in front of it into a wall of force. Distance had dissipated its effect, but it was nevertheless deadly. It passed over Ardo and his battlesuit, shaking him through the armor until he thought his teeth would be dislodged.

It would only be a moment, he knew. Either way, it would only be a moment.

Then the moment passed . . . and he was still there.

Ardo staggered to his feet.

The outpost that had been Oasis was hidden beneath the roiling red cloud—probably *was* the roiling red cloud, Ardo realized. The line of Zerg had not had any warning. Most were dead from the shock wave. Those few who remained seemed either confused or blind from the flash.

This certainly was no time to question which.

"Move it, Marines!" Breanne whooped. "Let's get home before these Zerg pigs figure out what happened!"

Ardo grabbed the handle on the battered metal case and turned, grinning, toward Sergeant Littlefield. "That was one amazing rescue, eh, Sarge?"

"Is that what that was?" To Ardo's astonishment, Littlefield's face was grim. "Let's get this box home. I need a shower and my bunk."

CHAPTER 11

HOMECOMING

THEY DRAGGED THEMSELVES OVER THE CREST OF the Basin wall. It was a site Ardo had wondered if he would see again. The walls of Scenic Outpost, dark in the failing light, thrust up out of the sandstone. Beyond its walls lay bunks, showers, meals, and, most of all, some measure of security. The Command Center towered over it all, beckoning Ardo like a siren. Its flashing beacons were so beautiful that it almost moved the Marine to tears.

Breanne straightened them all up on the ridge. It would not do to have them straggle in like a bunch of whipped dogs, she said. She formed them up, admonished them in no uncertain terms to keep themselves tall and proud or she would personally insert something unnatural into their anatomy that would force them to stand up straight. Then, with snap and precision, she marched them toward the garrison's deployment gate. Their fear of her overwhelmed their tiredness. What remained of the detail approached the compound like some sort of dust-caked military parade. If Breanne had had a flag, Ardo was certain she would have been waving it by now.

Ardo afforded himself a single backward glance. The great atomic cloud was dissipating over the Basin, its angry glow spreading eastward over the red mountains beyond. It had been an airburst: a detonation at a designated altitude that slammed down like a fist on anything beneath. The result was heavier physical damage but also a much lower radioactive fallout rate than from a ground detonation. Still, Ardo wondered if anyone had mentioned these facts to any settlers who might be remaining downwind of the deadly cloud's fallout. Most likely not, he decided. The Zerg are probably all that remain east of here anyway.

Their formation was much smaller than it had been earlier in the day. Ardo counted heads as they marched. The platoon of Marines was down by about half. Ekart, the second Firebat from his own squad, was missing and presumably either shredded or smashed flat on the floor of the Basin somewhere around Oasis. The same fate apparently had been visited upon Collins and Esson.

At least he hoped they were dead. It was entirely possible, he realized, that for some of them the nuke had blown the Zergs off them and welded the seals in the battle armor, but not completely crushed them in the blast wave. Sealed inside your own battle armor, unable to move on an abandoned, radioactive plain . . . The aching in his head was returning. Probably best not to think about it.

So it was another glorious day for the Confederacy Marines. Half their number had been left behind, but Ardo knew the mission would be chalked up as victorious. No, he realized, it was more than half. The Vulture cycles had not waited for them to return, but he recalled they had lost all but two before they had fled Oasis, and he did not actually know if either of them had survived to reach the garrison.

Glorious. All for a little metal box banging incessantly against his thigh and a single civilian draped over Cutter like a broken doll.

Breanne and the remains of her squad marched up to the east gate with all the dignity they could muster. A vibrant rust-colored sunset silhouetted the dark metallic walls of the garrison compound. There was something unnatural as they approached, something Ardo could not put a name to in his mind. As they approached the main lock, however, Breanne must have sensed something, too. She suddenly held up her left fist. The Marines all stopped at once, wary.

Breanne stood there for a moment. Ardo could not tell if the lieutenant was concerned or simply undecided.

"Breanne to Scenic Ops," she called over the com channel.

Silence. That was it, Ardo realized. He had not heard anything over the com channel but their own chatter as they approached the wall.

"Breanne to Scenic Ops. Respond, please."

The wind was picking up in the evening, the sound of the blowing sand hissing around their helmets. Ardo looked at the low bunkers set on either side of the lock. The dark slits had been comforting a few moments before. He had imagined each filled with sentry troops prepared to defend them against any assault. Now they seemed ominously empty and dark. He tried to see if there was any movement beyond the black slits, but it was impossible to tell.

The Marines glanced uneasily at each other.

The com channel crackled slightly.

Breanne signaled the platoon to ready weapons. It was not until that moment that Ardo realized he was without his gauss rifle. He felt suddenly quite vulnerable. He glanced accusingly at Littlefield, still holding the other handle on the metal box between them. Littlefield took no notice, his eyes shifting over the darkening walls of the garrison.

"Why don't they answer?"

"Could be a com problem."

"*Could* be? What if it ain't?"

Breanne stepped up to the keypad entry panel next to the massive, sealed gate. It took her several attempts before she managed a proper sequence the gate would accept.

Ardo felt it more than heard it. The massive gate through the garrison main lock groaned slowly upward. Breanne raised her weapon but held her ground. The others in the platoon followed her lead.

"Mellish, Bernelli, on point! Move!"

The two Marines hesitated only a moment, then moved quickly forward, gauss assault rifles held high. Each took up a position on either side of the darkened lock, peering in over their gun sights.

"Clear, Lieutenant!" Mellish called with a decided lack of conviction.

The inner door of the lock began to grind open as well. Its mass rose slowly, revealing the center of the garrison compound beyond bathed in the deepening rust of the sunset.

"Lieutenant?" Bernelli asked with a nervous edge to his voice.

"Hold your ground, Private!" Breanne stepped forward, her eyes trying to see beyond the narrow lock opening. "Cover us. Xiang, you're with me."

Breanne stepped into the lock, followed by the private. Both were swallowed at once by the dark corridor, their outlines etched against the deepening red of the compound clearing beyond. Just as quickly both figures stepped back into the light as they left the confines of the lock.

"Everyone, move up," Breanne called. "Quickly, people!"

Ardo glanced once more at Littlefield. The old veteran nodded, and they quickly moved forward with the rest of the platoon.

The clearing beyond the lock was not much more than a rally point set amid the too closely spaced buildings of the garrison. The Confederacy liked to keep their military bases tight and efficient: the smaller the area, the easier it is to apply resources and the less terrain you have to guard. At least, that was the doctrine engrained in all their commanders. The result was often a crowded hodgepodge of structures built far enough apart so that ground vehicles could maneuver between them. When fully staffed, this made any Confederacy garrison like an anthill, its narrow passages teeming with Marines, support personnel, and command staff all in a hurry to get somewhere.

Stepping hesitantly out of the lock space, Ardo noted once more that Scenic Garrison had been deployed like every other base he had ever served in, with one very notable exception.

No one was home.

The lock entered the clearing through the east side perimeter wall. The clearing itself had served as the landing area for the Dropships. Several buildings crowded in on the marginal open space. A ragged line of supply depots had been constructed in a tightly fitted puzzle on both the north and south sides of the clearing. A matching pair of missile turrets rose above them on either side. Their deployment heads still rotated as their homing systems searched automatically. To the west of the clearing, directly across from the lock, stood the three barracks units they had so casually left that same morning. A wide passage just to the south led back to the massive Command Center, the top of which could be seen towering above the barracks. The upper parts of the factory center and machine shop could just be made out farther beyond. A pair of SCVs stood next to a stack of supply containers on the north side of the clearing. Everything was exactly where it should have been.

"Mellish, cycle the lock." The lieutenant's voice was calm and quiet. Ardo used to talk the same way to the horses on his father's farm to calm them down when they were skittish. "Let's get that door closed. No sense being surprised from behind."

"Yeah," someone muttered over the com channel. "Especially since we got plenty to surprise us in front."

"That's enough, Bernelli." Breanne's voice remained ice calm. "You get that door closed yet, Mellish?"

"Yes, sir. Lock's secure."

"It's like they all just got up and left," Xiang muttered.

"Yeah," Littlefield agreed, "but look: I can see them leaving the supply huts and turrets—those are all built here—but the barracks are mobile. Hell, even the Command Center flies itself on those repulsor pads. They're all mobile units, and still in good repair by the looks of 'em. If they were evacuating, why not take the hardware, too?"

"All good questions, but what we need are answers." Breanne had made her decision. "Let's sweep the area. There may be people trapped or hurt or otherwise unable to communicate. Something's happened here, and whoever you run into is probably going to be a little nervous."

"You got *that* right!"

"Just take it easy and relax your trigger a little, got that? I don't want anybody blowing holes through our own just because we don't know what's going on. Littlefield and Melnikov, stay with me. Cutter, how's that civvy doing?"

"She's starting to come around, Lieutenant." Cutter held the woman cradled in both arms now. Against the massive islander, the woman looked tiny and frail, but Ardo could see she was stirring. "You want me to put her down?"

"No, there's an aid station in the Command Center." Breanne was frustrated. There was not much left for her to command. "Let's do this together. We'll start with the north barracks and then—"

"Lieutenant, I've got movement!"

"Where, Bernelli?"

"Looks like about fifty meters at about two-seven-eight degrees."

"That's the Command Center! Track it, Bernelli. Stay sharp, people!"

Bernelli's voice was rising ever so slightly in pitch as he spoke. "Tracking . . . moving south."

"We're in the open here, Lieutenant," Littlefield breathed.

Breanne understood at once. "Deploy forward! Take positions under the northern barracks. Use the landing struts for cover. Move!"

The platoon dashed quickly across the clearing. Ardo ran awkwardly next to Littlefield, the two of them still struggling with the metal box between them. Ardo fleetingly thought about the supply huts just a few meters away from him. Within one of them would be a brand-new rifle for him and a fresh supply of ammo. Instead, here he crouched, cowering in the landing well of a mobile barracks with nothing to defend himself except harsh language, spit, and this stupid metal box which, as far as he was concerned, could have stayed in Oasis and become part of the great radiant cloud drifting off to the east.

"Bernelli?" Breanne spoke quietly, despite the fact that the battle armor kept her words restricted to the com channel.

"Still tracking, Lieutenant. Moving fast. Fifteen meters on the two hundred radial. Maintaining an eastern line."

"It's coming down the road," Littlefield rumbled.

"Fifteen meters still. Should be able to see it . . ."

Ardo crouched lower behind the strut.

A single figure, bathed in the dying light of the day, staggered out into the clearing.

"Oh, *shit!*" Breanne spat. She stood up, snapping back the faceplate of her battle armor and yelling across the clearing. "Marcus, what in the name of *hell* are you doing?"

The figure turned. His fatigues were no longer crisp or clean. He had lost his snappy hat, revealing a head of straw hair that seemed to stick out in directions of its own free will. Nevertheless, Ardo recognized him as the technician who had joined them on the flight out to Scenic just yesterday.

"Ma'am, oh!" Sergeant Marcus Jans snapped to a ridgid salute. "Welcome home, ma'am!"

Lieutenant Breanne returned the salute casually, then asked, "Permission to enter the garrison?"

"Uh, ma'am?"

"I assume you are in charge of this post, Sergeant, or someone else would have greeted us by now."

"Oh." Jans seemed confused. "Yes, ma'am, I guess I am . . . except for you . . . now, I mean."

Ardo was suddenly reminded of his cat and the mouse once more.

"Then I'm reporting my platoon as having returned from a glorious mission on behalf of the Confederacy." Breanne's voice was tired and her temper was starting to give it an edge.

Jans looked past Breanne to where Ardo and his companions had taken cover. "You mean, the Marines hiding under the barracks?"

"So much for our glorious return," Cutter rumbled.

"Yes." Breanne spoke the words through her teeth. "The Marines hiding under the barracks are asking permission to enter your garrison, Sergeant, and then I want to know where the *hell* the *garrison has gone!*"

Jans blinked as Breanne's final words seemed to rock him back on his heels.

"But . . . but, Lieutenant . . . I thought *you* could tell *me!*"

CHAPTER 12

GHOST TOWN

"WHAT THE *HELL* ARE YOU TALKING ABOUT, TIN-ker?" Breanne was in no mood to guess. The wrath in her voice might just melt the technical sergeant right down into his scuffed boots.

"Well, ma'am, they just all pulled out," Marcus stammered. The dirt on the sergeant's face was marred by the streaks of sweat starting to run down from his hairline. "I thought, you being in the command loop and all, you'd know about it, that's all."

Littlefield stepped toward Breanne and the tech sergeant, dragging Ardo closer by virtue of the metal box still hanging between them. He spoke in a low voice, confidentially, but Ardo was too close to avoid hearing. "Lieutenant, it's getting dark, and we've got no place else to hide."

Breanne's gaze had been locked with building fury on Jans but Littlefield's words somehow penetrated her rage. Her head snapped up, and she seemed to be seeing the fading sky for the first time above the dim walls of the garrison.

"We probably don't have a lot of time," Littlefield whispered toward the ground, but the words were meant for the lieutenant.

"The post has been abandoned," Breanne announced suddenly. "Some sort of SNAFU is my guess. I'll get it straightened out. Meanwhile, Cutter . . ."

"Yes, ma'am."

"There's an aid station in the Command Center. Take that woman there, strap her to a bunk, and then report back to me. Littlefield, take Melnikov and go with Cutter. Have Melnikov keep an eye on that treasure chest of yours and the woman—if he can handle it."

"He'll do fine, Lieutenant. I'll see to it."

"Well, would you also 'see to it' that he gets a new rifle, and pick one up for yourself while you're at it." Breanne's lips very nearly smiled. "Then get back here to me. We've got to set up a perimeter."

Cutter grunted once and shifted the position of the moaning woman still in his arms. There was disappointment in his voice as he spoke. "Not much fun tonight, Lieutenant. We just nuked the Zerg into bloody little bits. All that's left now is to call for the bus to take us out. War's all finished here." The big man shook his head sadly. "No, ma'am, not much fun tonight at all."

Littlefield glanced at Breanne, but if he was looking for any reaction, he did not get the satisfaction.

"You have your orders." The lieutenant spoke with an even chill. Then she turned back to the tech sergeant. "As for you, Sergeant Jans, you stay with me. I have a lot of questions for you, and I don't want you getting lost before I can ask them."

Night was falling quickly as they made their way to the infirmary. The wind had picked up considerably from the west, its sounds moaning and wailing among the buildings of the Confederacy garrison compound. Ardo shuddered at the sound. The deserted buildings seemed to stare back at him as he moved between them. The place was altogether too still for the massive amount of equipment remaining here. Everywhere he looked he was greeted by visions of things that were entirely in place and yet somehow wrong. The ground beneath his feet was packed hard under the treads and repulsors of various vehicles that had trod over it. The bright lights still burned in each of the modules as they passed. One supply depot access door was open, its interior work lights spilling into the street. An SCV loader stood within, its vaguely humanoid metal-and-plastic shape poised to pick up a shipping module. Its operator, however, was long gone, like a spirit who had abandoned its physical body in death. Everywhere he looked, there were the bootprints of Marines and technicians who should have been walking over that same ground still, but were somehow missing. Now they only existed here as ghosts. Ardo was not sure whether he would be more surprised by actually seeing someone else or by the constant strain of *not* seeing anyone at all.

The main access roadway wound around the back of the southern barracks module, curving across the flattened ground toward the hulking Command Center. The building was massive, as wide as it was tall, the suggestion of a flattened metallic spheroid in its general shape. It had obviously been built for function rather than aesthetics. Some Confederacy technical draftsman back at R&D Division probably had an impassioned affair with this design at one point, but he was alone in his appreciation. The Command Center was all business. Massive repulsor landing claws supported the main bulk of the structure, their thick struts disappearing into wide housing cowls. External ablative plates reinforced the armored hull. Above that, at a level three stories higher than the ground, a variety of observation towers, antennae, sensor domes and other technical gadgetry were arranged in what appeared to the casual observer to be utter chaos. Above it all sat the Operations Center, an armored block with windows on all sides that lorded over the entire complex. The lights were shining brightly from those windows, but there was no movement behind them as far as Ardo could see.

The main access ramp to the Command Center had been lowered, the hydraulic arms fully extended to either side. The main command bay was well lit, but Ardo could not help but feel that they were all walking into the mouth of some great, dark beast.

The brightness of the bay helped, however, once they were inside its glow. The fewer shadows the better. The main bay towered over them through two decks. To his left and right, Ardo knew that the Command Center held the mineral and gas processors, which were the heart that sustained any mobile command base. Their bulk took up most of the Command Center's internal space.

Overhead, squeezed into a space between the massive processors, was the SCV maintenance bay. "Maintenance" was something of a misnomer: the fabricators on that level could create an SCV from scratch just using the mineral processor output alone. Several T-280 Space Construction Vehicles hung suspended from their construction racks overhead. They swayed slightly. Ardo had to remind himself that it was probably the ventilation system moving the suits.

He noticed his annoying headache had returned. Littlefield continued forward toward the lift at the end of the bay. Ardo kept up with him as he held the metal case. They both turned as they stepped onto the lift platform. Cutter, still cradling the woman in his arms, joined them, and then Littlefield activated the lift.

As they rose, Ardo tried to get a better look at the woman. The massive tangle of her long, filthy hair was his first and strongest impression. Her face was turned away from him, toward Cutter's chest. She wore the ubiquitous jumpsuit of a colonist worker, probably a worker in the engineering or waterfarm projects out in Oasis. The sole of one of her boots was partially torn away from the top leather. It struck him as an odd thing, considering everything else that must have happened to her companions down in that outpost town.

At least, now that the town was drifting in a glowing cloud to the east, they would not need to go in and clean up the dead.

Clean up the dead?

The phrase caught in his mind, but he could not attach any significance to it. Besides, his head hurt too much to think about it much more. Better to just get on with the current task and forget about it.

The lift quickly rose into the overhead shaft, then stopped at Level 3. Cutter turned with the woman and carried her down the narrow hall. It was a difficult feat, especially in the huge Firebat armor, but Cutter managed it without much trouble. He seemed to wear the armor like a second skin.

"Let's go," Littlefield urged with a nudge against the box that carried into Ardo's thigh. Ardo shook himself from his own thoughts and began moving down the corridor.

The infirmary was well encased by the rest of the Command Center. It was situated nearly in the exact middle of the structure. There were no regen tanks here or really much of anything that citizens of the Confederacy might consider standard equipment for a medical facility. The infirmary was more of a first-aid station, a stopping place on the journey of an injured

Marine to keep him just alive enough so that he could reach better care and facilities.

There were several bunks mounted against one wall. Most of these were neatly and crisply made up in the traditional Marine style. One, however, was in disarray, its sheets dropping casually toward the floor.

Cutter entered the room, his bulk seeming to take up most of it. He found a middle bunk that seemed to suit his requirements and lay the groaning woman down. The big man finally was able to flip open his helmet faceplate just as Ardo and Littlefield entered the room. Ardo could see the sweat streaming down the islander's brown face.

"That wasn't good," he huffed. He quickly released the locking rings on his gloves and pulled his hands free. In moments he was strapping the bed restraints around the listless woman's hands, chest, and feet. "Need more exercise. Gotta work out more."

Ardo smiled and shook his head. Cutter had just run several kilometers with that woman either on his back or in his arms. Even with the help of the suit, that was a remarkable performance. Ardo smiled to think that Cutter would consider it a sign of weakness.

Littlefield motioned Ardo over to the right. Against the opposite wall from the bunks, a desk stood away from the wall with a chair on its far side.

Littlefield stopped. "Will you look at that!"

Ardo and Littlefield both stopped.

The desk was clean and uncluttered except for a

partially downed cup of coffee and a half-eaten sandwich.

Cutter gazed at it as well for a moment, then he reached forward with his massive right hand and picked up the cup.

"Still warm," he said, then downed the coffee in a single gulp.

Ardo and Littlefield stared at him, amazed.

"Needed sugar," Cutter reflected as he gathered up the remains of the sandwich and began stuffing it into his mouth. The rest of his words were barely discernible through the bread. "I'm heading out. You two need anything, just shout. I'm sure *someone* will come."

Cutter grabbed his battle gloves and stepped out of the room, the infirmary door sliding closed behind him.

Littlefield returned Ardo's astonished look, then both men broke into a hearty laugh.

"Unbelievable," Ardo gasped between laughs.

"No, not really," Littlefield responded with good nature. "He's really not that bad once you get to know him."

Ardo sat down in the desk chair, not an easy thing to do in his battle suit. "You know him?"

"Sure," Littlefield said as he sat on the edge of the desk. "He served under me for a while. Our styles didn't mesh very well. I guess my style didn't mesh very well with a lot of people."

Ardo could not think of anything to say in the silence that followed.

"Well," Littlefield went on, looking away, "it's a nice infirmary but you *are* on duty. Guard duty now that I think of it. Here's the box—whatever the hell it's supposed to be—and I don't think that woman will give you any trouble. Still, keep on the com channel, and whatever you do, stay awake! I'll go find us a couple of nice new rifles and fresh ammo. Breanne wants to set the watches, then we'll see about some chow. I'll be back before you know it."

"Sure, Sarge," Ardo nodded. He had not realized how tired he was until he sat down. "I hear you."

Littlefield smiled. "Head still bothering you?"

Ardo nodded slightly. "A little."

"I guess the resoc is taking after all. And hey, you're a veteran now! You've made your first kill and survived to tell about it."

The Zergling twitched before him. The beast's dull, black eye stared back at him.

"And God said, Let the waters bring forth abundantly the moving creature that hath life . . ."

Ardo could not breathe.

Ardo frowned suddenly and looked away. "Yes, sir."

Littlefield frowned slightly. "You're going to be all right, kid. I won't be long."

The sergeant stood up and walked purposefully toward the door. The door obliged him, slipping out of his way and then closing once he had passed.

Ardo took a deep breath.

There was nothing for him to do but wait. He could

imagine nothing worse than to be left with his own thoughts.

"I'll never leave you behind," he said to her. *The wheat rustled about the blanket where they lay.*

He was falling into her luminescent blue eyes.

Golden . . .

Ardo stood up. There had to be something he could do. His head was throbbing once again.

The woman on the bunk was apparently not faring much better. She was starting to struggle dazedly against the restraints, her moans increasing.

Ardo quickly started searching through the wall cabinets of the infirmary. He wet down a towel in the wall basin and moved over toward the woman.

"Easy, lady," Ardo spoke in soothing tones. "Nobody is going to hurt you."

The woman's head flailed from side to side beneath her nimbus of matted, tangled hair. Her struggles were getting more pronounced by the moment.

"Hey . . . look, lady, you've got to relax! We're here to help you." It was not working. Ardo grabbed the woman by the shoulders and shook her. "Stop it! Listen to me!"

The woman suddenly stopped struggling.

"You're safe now," Ardo sighed as he released her shoulders. He took up the wetted towel again and moved to brush aside the hair covering the woman's face. "You're in the Confederacy Garrison at Scenic. No one is going to . . ."

His voice trailed off.

Golden.

He blinked, then shook.

The woman stared at him from the bunk.

The nimbus of her long shining hair played softly in the warm, gentle breeze drifting over the wheat field.

Tears welled up unbidden in Ardo's eyes. "Melani? Melani! It's you! My God, it's a miracle! A miracle!"

Overwhelmed, Ardo clasped the woman's head lovingly in his hands.

He drew his lips close to hers.

The woman screamed.

CHAPTER 13

MERDITH

ARDO JUMPED BACKWARD AS THOUGH HIT BY AN electric shock. His head was pounding. "Melani! Please, stop! It's me!"

The woman screamed again, her eyes wide with fright.

Ardo held his hands up, trying to will her to calm down. His eyes stung, filling with tears. His head throbbed, almost blinding him as well. "Please! I won't hurt you. You're confused . . . and . . . and hurt. It's been so long, I . . ."

"*Get away from me, you bastard!*" The woman's teeth chattered as she struggled to control her fear. "Where the hell am I?"

"You're in the infirmary at . . . uh . . . at . . ." Ardo winced against the pain exploding in his skull. He was finding it hard to think. "At the Scenic Garrison . . . on Mar Sara. It's a Confederacy outpost base . . ."

She struggled against the restraining straps once more, rattling the framework of the wall-mounted cot. Cutter had done his job well. In a few moments, exhausted, she lay back panting.

"Please, Melani." Ardo blinked back tears. He struggled with the lock rings on his gloves, desperate to remove them, as he spoke. "If only you knew how much I've dreamed of this . . . how much I longed for you. I've seen your face a thousand times in the crowd . . ."

She turned her face toward him, still blinking, struggling to remain conscious. "This is a Confederacy base?"

"Yes!" Anguish in his face, Ardo stepped toward her. "Oh, Melani, if you only knew how sorry I am . . ."

The woman yelled at him with all her strength. *"Take one more step you sonofabitch and I'll kill you!"*

Ardo stopped, frozen, unable to move forward or retreat. The thundering pain in his head overwhelmed him. He gave a single, choked cry and collapsed to the floor, sobbing uncontrollably. Memories washed and flooded across his mind. Golden fields. Golden hair. Screams and crimson blood.

It was some time before he heard her voice, quietly talking to him.

"Hey, soldier-boy, it's all right. Relax, it's gonna be fine."

Ardo looked up through the blur of his tears.

"Just take it easy, okay? We'll talk . . . just talk . . . all right? I'll help you make it better. Deal?"

Ardo nodded slowly. He was spent, sitting ignominiously in his battlesuit on the floor of the infirmary, his back propped against the desk.

"That's fine." The woman's voice was calm and deliberate, as though she were talking a suicide away from the edge of a cliff. "You just sit there and we'll talk for a minute and get all this sorted out, okay?"

Ardo nodded vaguely again.

"My name is Merdith. What's yours?"

Ardo sucked in a ragged breath.

"Look at me."

Ardo did not know if he had the strength. "Oh, Melani . . ."

"Look at me," Merdith said a little more forcefully.

Ardo raised his eyes.

"Look at me closely." Merdith lay still, concentrating her dark eyes on Ardo's face. "Look at my hair . . . look at it. Is that, uh, Melani's hair?"

Ardo struggled to concentrate.

"Look at it . . . see it. Is that Melani's hair?"

The hair was different. It was obviously much darker, even without the dirt. Melani's hair was so beautifully fine and . . .

"My eyes," Merdith ordered once more. "Are these Melani's eyes?"

Ardo shifted and gazed into the woman's dark, almost black eyes. They were like deep pools in a cavern. Melani's own eyes were such a brilliant blue . . .

Ardo looked away. "No . . . those are not Melani's eyes."

"Hello. My name is Merdith," the woman tried quietly once more. "What's yours?"

"Ardo . . . Ardo Meln . . . Private Ardo Melnikov, ma'am." Ardo still could not look at the woman on the bunk. "I'm . . . so very sorry, ma'am. I don't know what happened to me. Please . . . accept my apologies."

"It's all right, soldier, no harm done." Merdith looked up at the ceiling, considering before she spoke. "You're a resoc, aren't you?"

"Ma'am?" The throbbing in Ardo's head had left for a moment but was making a definite comeback.

"A resoc—neural resocialization—training through memory overlay, right?"

"Yes . . . I guess that makes me a 're-sock' or whatever you call it." Ardo was suddenly very tired again. "Look, ma'am, I said I was sorry for what I did and I meant it. Now . . . well, maybe it's just better we didn't talk anymore."

He gathered up his battle gloves and pushed himself up from the floor. He still could not bring himself to look at her again. He moved back around to the other side of the desk, trying hard to be alone.

But he was never alone, especially now. The ghosts in his mind continued to torment him. The thought of sitting down and waiting for Littlefield to come back was torment. He needed something else to think about, something else to occupy his mind than the black idle thoughts that were always a moment away from overwhelming him.

The metal case sat before him.

The treasure that had nearly gotten him killed—had killed others already.

There was a puzzle to occupy his mind. The case had two handles on either side. What appeared to be the top was held down by six separate latching mechanisms. They were not locked—which seemed to Ardo to be reasonable enough invitation to open them.

He reached forward and snapped open the first latch.

"I, uh, I wouldn't do that if I were you."

Ardo looked up. Merdith was still strapped to the bunk. She was speaking to Ardo, but her eyes were on the box.

"Why not?" Ardo asked in a flat tone.

"Well . . . you might not want to know what's inside."

Ardo snorted, then snapped open a second latch.

Merdith started visibly.

"I'm serious, soldier-boy."

"I'm sure you are," Ardo sighed, idly snapping open the third latch.

Merdith's voice rose slightly in pitch and urgency. "There's an ancient earth legend about this woman named Pandora. You ever hear about that, soldier-boy?"

"Yes," Ardo answered irritably. He was having trouble with the fourth latch. It seemed to be stuck. "We're not all bumpkins in the colonies, you know. I studied mythology in school."

Ardo grunted, and the fourth latch swung open.

"Is that where you met her?" Merdith asked quickly. "Is that where you met Melani?"

Ardo stopped. "What the *hell* are you talking about, lady?"

"Melani, I'm asking about Melani." Merdith licked her lips nervously. "I just . . . I just wanted to know where you met her, that's all."

"Look, uh . . ."

"Merdith. I'm Merdith."

"Yeah. Look, Merdith, that was a long time ago on a planet you probably never heard of and probably couldn't care less about even if you *had* heard of it." Ardo shook his head, looking for the next latch. "It just doesn't matter anymore."

"What happened there?" Merdith pressed on. "What happened to Melani?"

Sharp pain flashed behind Ardo's right eye. He winced.

"Tell me . . . tell me what happened to her."

He saw her behind him. The Zerg were pressing their attack with anger now. The Dropship was depriving them of their prize. Ardo was appalled at how quickly the large crowd had been sundered—harvested like blood-red wheat in the field. The Zerg were already nearly at Melani's side.

Ardo shuddered. "It doesn't matter . . . You shouldn't ask . . ."

"I want to know," she pressed him. "What do you remember, soldier-boy? What do you see in your mind?"

They were already nearly at Melani's side.

Ardo clawed and fought. He screamed.

Three Hydralisks grasped Melani at once, dragging her back from the edge of the crowd.

"What do you *see*?"

"Leave me alone!"

"Please, Ardo!" she wept. "Don't leave me alone!"

The mindless mob pushed him farther into the ship.

Merdith urged again. "Tell me!"

"She's dead, all right?" Ardo raged. "She's dead! The Zerg attacked our settlement. The Confederacy came to evac us and I tried to save her and I failed, okay? I tried . . . I tried to get her into the Dropship but the crowd was between us . . . and I . . . and I couldn't . . . I just couldn't . . ."

Ardo's voice trailed off. To his surprise, he saw his own sadness mirrored in Merdith's eyes.

"Oh, soldier-boy," she spoke quietly. "Is that what they told you? Is that what you believe?"

The com channel chimed in his headpiece, the sound carrying into the room. Somewhere in Ardo's mind he recognized it but could not bring himself to answer its call.

"I'm so sorry for you, soldier-boy."

The com channel chimed once more. What was this woman trying to tell him?

The com channel chimed a third time.

"You gonna answer that?" Merdith asked.

Ardo shook himself from his confused thoughts and toggled the com to Open Vox. "Melnikov here."

"Littlefield here. You all right up there, son?"

Merdith continued to keep her eyes on Ardo. The Marine had become more than a little suspicious of the woman. He stepped back around the desk, and hopefully out of range for the woman to overhear the com channel.

"Yes, sergeant, we're just fine here."

"Are we, indeed? Well, I've found us a pair of very clean and very new Impaler C-14's fresh out of storage for us both. I'll be with you directly. What's the condition of your prisoner?"

"She's talkative," Ardo replied, drawing a wry smile from the woman.

"Well, let's hope she remains that way. The lieutenant wants both her and that box brought up to Operations as soon as I join you. I'm at the Command Center entrance now. Littlefield out."

Ardo toggled the com channel to Standby once more and quickly began closing the latches on the box.

"I hope we'll get a chance to talk again, soldier-boy." Merdith's words were silken. "I know something about Melani's fate that you really should be told."

"You couldn't possibly know anything about it."

"But I do."

"Like what?"

"That it's all a lie, soldier-boy. It's all a lie."

CHAPTER 14

DIMINISHING RETURNS

"HEY, MELNIKOV! THE LIEUTENANT WANTS US UP at Operations on the—Melnikov, you all right?"

Ardo had barely noticed Littlefield moving through the door. He was still staring at Merdith, his eyes narrowing. "What did you just say?"

Littlefield mistook Ardo's words as being meant for him. "I said the lieutenant wants us up at Operations. Lose something?"

The sergeant tossed a new C-14 gauss rifle to Ardo. Feeling its weight in his hand was reassuring. Without thinking, Ardo checked the breach, noted the load count on the clip, and armed the weapon. It felt good to be doing something mindless.

"How's the woman?" The sergeant carefully set his own new weapon on top of the metal case, then walked quickly over to the bunk where Merdith remained bound. "Oh, I see you're awake, ma'am. How are you feeling?"

"Restrained," Merdith answered flatly.

Littlefield laughed to himself as he checked the dilation of her eyes. "Well, I see you haven't lost any humor. Anything broken? Anything sprained?"

"I'm portable," Merdith responded.

"Yeah, but I'll bet you're hard to move," Littlefield chuckled as he leaned back. "All right, miss, I'm going to let you loose now. The lieutenant wants to have a few words with you. There's nothing to worry about—we just pulled you out of a bad spot and this is just routine, you understand?"

Merdith nodded.

"So you aren't going to give me any trouble, are you?"

"And if I did?" Merdith sniffed.

"Well, we both have very big guns, ma'am."

"That's what they all say," Merdith laughed in turn. "I won't be any trouble, Sergeant, and I very much want to talk to your lieutenant. I'll be polite."

"Now that's what I like to hear," Littlefield said pleasantly as he began undoing the restraining straps from the bunk. "I'm sure we'll all be really good friends as soon as we get a few things cleared up. Isn't that right, Melnikov?"

"Sir, yes, sir." Ardo responded automatically. Somewhere inside the depths of his brain he was not all that certain.

Littlefield undid the nearest ankle strap last and then took a large step back.

"Frightened?" Merdith said as she sat up.

"Cautious, ma'am," Littlefield replied as he reached

back behind him and took his weapon. "Just cautious."

"How about your treasure chest over there?" Merdith's voice seemed casual to Ardo in a very studied, dangerous sort of way. "Does it get to come with us?"

"Why is that any concern of yours?" Littlefield's eyes narrowed.

"I've been baby-sitting that little crate for quite a while now. Let's just say we've gotten to be quite attached to each other." Merdith slid off the side of the bunk, carefully trying to stand. Her left foot bent over wrong, however, and she had to catch herself before she fell.

"Hurt, ma'am?" Littlefield asked.

"Just the pride." Merdith lifted her foot to examine the ruined boot. She shook her head. "And these were my favorite pair, too. Well, as my mother used to say, 'Make do or do without.' You think you can find me some duct tape around here somewhere, Sarge?"

"Duct tape?" Littlefield laughed. "Isn't that a bit old-fashioned?"

"Ask an engineer," Merdith said as she limped toward the infirmary door. "You can fix anything with duct tape."

The Operations Room was situated at the very top of the Command Center. The Great Designer—whoever he was—had decided to make it into a large box with sloped armor and a ring of transsteel windows running around the entire room. An officer could see in all directions through those windows by walking along a raised platform that ringed the room on all four sides.

The centerpiece of the Operations Room, however, was the command island, a raised circular platform situated in the center of the room. From here the central command staff could monitor activities not only through the windows beyond but at the various stations around the Operations Room.

Command consoles were situated on the underside of the walkway platform as well as on the command island. These could monitor nearly every aspect of operations that a remote base of the Confederacy might be called upon to perform. They were rarely ever used all at once. They only had their transport covers removed when the demands of the base's mission required them. It was said that one could get a good feel for what a base was tasked to accomplish just by knowing which consoles had been uncovered for use.

As the lift platform brought Ardo, Merdith, and Littlefield up into the Operations Room, Ardo was struck by the number of consoles still secured under their transport covers. He had not been in Scenic long enough to get more than a limited look at the base— just the barracks, actually, before they set out on the morning mission. As he stepped off the lift with Littlefield, a quick glance around told him that there really wasn't much more to the base than just the barracks. There was a factory console open with its machine shop console next to it as well. They could make basic things here, apparently, but not much more. A single supply station was uncovered, too. He was more interested in what was missing: those consoles that were still covered and never pressed into service. Armory, Engineering, and Starport support were all still sealed. More important, the refinery controls remained locked up, meaning that they had no means of producing their own gas to power any larger pieces of equipment. All they could rely on would be whatever remained in the depot stores. At least there was one console he was just as glad was still secure: there apparently was no Academy here, either.

Not much to work with, Ardo reflected. *Why is this base even here?* he wondered.

Lieutenant Breanne stood hunched over the command table on the island. Cutter stood nearby, intent on Breanne's instructions as she pointed at the surface display on the table.

"The perimeter fencing extends only about three-quarters of the way around the base. It ends here . . . and here . . ."—Breanne pointed again at the display—"at the top of this cliff face. There's about a thirty-foot drop straight down and then another twenty feet of loose dirt and rock to the base of the ravine. The face is sandstone—pretty slick stuff even for the Zerg. The ravine empties down into the Basin, most of which is a nuclear slag pile now. I don't expect 'em from this direction, but I don't exactly want to be surprised by them either."

"Lieutenant?" Littlefield spoke up.

Breanne did not look up from the display as she spoke. "Yes, thank you, Sergeant. Cutter, get out to the perimeter. Have Xiang and Mellish give the defense towers a quick look to make sure they're all operating, then set the watch as we discussed."

"At your will, Lieutenant," Cutter replied with a stiff salute. He jumped down off the island, his heavy Firebat suit causing the floor plates to ring with the impact. His broad face flashed into a massive smile as he saw Merdith. "Well, Princess! Nice to see you with your eyes open!"

"Flattered, I'm sure," Merdith yawned.

"Hey, you should be. Not every woman gets to be rescued by Fetu Koura-Abi!" The huge islander thumped the chestplate of his Firebat suit, then rumbled as suavely as he could muster. "No need to thank me now. I'm sure you can think of better ways to thank me later!"

Merdith batted her eyes at him with exaggerated motion. "Gee, thanks for bringing me here, you big, strong Marine you!"

The sarcasm was completely lost on Cutter. "Hee-hee. You find me later and I'll take care of you better than ever."

Cutter strutted to the lift, missing completely Merdith's rolled eyes and soured face.

It was not, however, lost on Lieutenant Breanne,

who now stood facing them from the island with her arms folded across her chest. Her short-cropped hair seemed to bristle on its own. "My name is Lieutenant L. Z. Breanne of the Confederate Marines. And you are?"

Merdith eyed the lieutenant carefully, sizing her up. "I'm Merdith Jernic. I am . . . well, was . . . an engineer down at Oasis Station."

"An engineer?"

"Yes, that's what I said."

"And what did you engineer?"

"Thermal wells and condenser systems for the water supply."

"I see." Lieutenant Breanne stepped down from the island, her hands still folded across her chest. "And you were found in possession of that case."

"Well, I . . . don't know," Merdith replied levelly. "I believe I was unconscious at the time."

Breanne chuckled darkly. "How convenient for you."

"Well, ma'am, if you're about to be eaten by the Zerg, I certainly recommend being unconscious first."

Breanne's eyes leveled with Merdith's. "Do you know what is in that case?"

Merdith hesitated for a moment, then responded, "Do you?"

Breanne smiled thinly, then strode directly over to where Littlefield and Ardo still held the metallic box between them. "Let's find out."

"Wait," Merdith said quietly.

Breanne snapped open two of the latches in a swift move.

"Wait," Merdith spoke more insistently.

The lieutenant turned her icy eyes toward Merdith. "You have something to say."

Merdith licked her lips.

Breanne took two quick steps, her sharply angled face suddenly within inches of the civilian's. "What is so important in this case?"

Merdith looked away.

Breanne's voice was low and dangerous. "I've had a very long day, lady, and I don't have any intention of making it any longer. The Confederacy Marine Command sent me and my people here to retrieve this damn box . . . and I don't ask any questions. They drop me in the middle of some godforsaken planet in the outer colonies . . . and I don't ask any questions. Now that I've got the damn thing, I've been left here high and dry, my evac has deserted me, a tactical nuclear device drops behind me unannounced . . ."

Unannounced? Ardo thought. *The lieutenant had not even been warned of the incoming?*

". . . half my platoon is wasted dragging their asses out of this mess only to find my sortie base is suddenly a ghost town . . . and *now, now at last,* I have some questions. And you are going to answer them."

Merdith's eyes flashed with anger.

"What is in this case?"

"It's proof."

"Proof of what?"

"Proof that the Confederacy brought the Zerg to Mar Sara," Merdith snapped. "Proof that the Confederacy is developing a terrible weapon capable of destroying the civilian population on entire worlds."

Breanne let out a grunt of disbelief and walked back to the case. She once more began flipping open the latches. "So now you show up with a box full of papers and documents and other such 'proof' and expect me to believe—"

"Please, stop!" Merdith shouted.

Breanne pulled out her side arm in a single swift motion, leveling the muzzle between Merdith's eyebrows. "Why should I?"

"Because," Merdith spoke quietly, her voice as level as her eyes fixed on the lieutenant's gun, "that box contains the device that called the Zerg here. If you open it, you'll activate it, and every Zergling, Hydralisk, or Mutalisk within ten thousand clicks of this building will move heaven and earth to get into this very room."

"You're insane," Breanne murmured.

"No, ma'am," Merdith countered, her voice subdued. "With all due respect, I think you are describing the people who would build such a thing."

Ardo held his breath. He felt almost detached as he watched the exchange taking place not more than a meter in front of him.

Breanne's gun remained steady. "You stole this . . . this device?"

"No, ma'am, like I told you: I'm an engineer. Some members of the Sons of Korhal brought it to me for examination."

" 'Sons of Korhal'?" Littlefield tilted his head skeptically. "Who the hell are the 'Sons of Korhal'?"

"Damned if I know," Breanne sniffed. "Some local troublemakers, probably. Korhal is a planet in the core Confederacy worlds that rebelled some time ago. I think it was under quarantine blockade last time I heard anything about it. We've seen a lot of these lately—small, isolated rebel groups trying to undermine the integrity of the Confederacy."

"We're growing," Merdith sniffed proudly. "We may be small now, but soul by soul, house by house, planet by planet we threaten this so-called Confederacy."

"Terrorists," Breanne snapped.

"Revolutionaries," Merdith returned.

"Gnats with delusions of grandeur," Breanne snorted. "So these terrorists brought the box to you . . ."

Breanne's voice lowered to a whisper.

"And you opened it . . . didn't you?"

Merdith continued to gaze at the gun muzzle, but remained silent.

Breanne lowered her weapon and holstered it.

"Merdith Jernic, I'm placing you under custody

pending an investigation into the theft of Confederacy property."

Merdith smiled to herself as she shook her head. It struck Ardo as ludicrous to arrest the woman, but Breanne always seemed to do things by the book, regardless of how little sense it might make.

"I will investigate your statements and, if they are found to be substantially truthful, you will be released. Do you understand?"

Merdith nodded with a chuckle. "More than you may know."

"Littlefield, leave that 'evidence' here with me and escort this woman down to the barracks for some chow. Have her back here in an hour."

"Begging your pardon, ma'am," Ardo spoke up.

"You have something to contribute, Private?"

The iced steel eyes swung on Ardo, making him most uncomfortable. "Yes, ma'am. I'll take the duty, ma'am. I could use some chow myself and it might relieve the sergeant for more pressing duties."

"You're volunteering, Private?"

"Yes, ma'am . . . if it's quite all right."

Breanne shrugged. "Be my guest. Littlefield, find that Tech Sergeant Jans and get him up here. We'll see if we can get this puzzle put together. And, Melnikov . . ."

"Yes, ma'am?"

"Have her back here in one hour," the lieutenant

emphasized. "I want her none the worse for wear, but don't lose her."

"Yes, ma'am."

Ardo took Merdith by the arm and guided her toward the lift. The lieutenant may have no more questions, but Ardo had plenty of his own, and he had no intention of losing Merdith now.

CHAPTER 15

MIND'S EYE

ARDO PROPELLED THEM BOTH DOWN THE MAIN ramp of the Command Center and toward the nearest barracks entrance just to their left. The wind was howling out of the west, whipping the dry dirt in the compound. The whirls of sand whispered and moaned between the buildings. Ardo, still in his combat suit, was relatively unaffected by the gale. The woman next to him, however, was exposed to the elements. Her right arm held the lapel of her worker's coveralls across her face, her left arm still held firmly by the Marine.

Ardo was in a hurry to get her inside, and not because of her exposure to the weather.

They passed between the massive landing struts and repulsor pads of the southern barracks. A column of golden light poured from the access ramp, making it easy to find.

He loved the barracks, he thought suddenly, but wondered why they always made him feel queasy in the stomach. He did not take time to think about it, however: there was too much to think about as it was. Still holding Merdith's arm in a firm grip, he marched them both up the ramp and into the deployment room.

Deployment was one of the larger spaces in a very cramped arrangement. It sat at the top of the ramp and was used by Marines for staging. All around him there were weapons and equipment racks. Most were ordered and locked, although a few of the cabinets hung open. A maintenance kit sat on the floor in front of one of them. Someone apparently working on a battlesuit had just left it there.

The entire site had been abandoned, apparently without much notice. More questions. They made his head hurt, but he thought he might have some of the answers quite literally at hand.

"You all right, ma'am?" Ardo asked casually. "That wind is pretty awful tonight."

Merdith coughed a couple of times as she patted the dust off herself with her free hand. "That wind is pretty awful *every* night, soldier-boy. We're raised on sand here. It doesn't bother us." She sighed and then winced, looking up at Ardo through his faceplate. "Say, if I promise not to run away, do you think you could let go of my arm?"

Ardo blinked, letting go. "Oh, uh, yes, ma'am. You wouldn't do anything stupid, would you?"

"I promise I won't dance with anyone else all night." She smiled, then looked around for a moment.

There were numerous exits from the Ready Room that led deeper into the barracks. "So, where do you go around here to buy a girl a cup of coffee?"

"That hatchway on the right," Ardo gestured with the muzzle of his C-14. "You first. . . . I insist."

Merdith arched her eyebrows and smiled casually. Ardo smiled back, pressing open the visor on his combat suit with his free hand. Merdith nodded and moved ahead. The massive pressure door swung open easily.

Dim light illuminated the corridor beyond. The passage was lined with large transparent tubes. Each appeared to be filled with a blue-green liquid that circulated constantly. Monitors above each showed them to be in ready mode. Each had its own separate panel of controls, while at the end of the corridor to the left of another pressure door stood a raised control booth.

"By the gods," Merdith spoke almost reverently. "These are neural resocialization chambers, aren't they? These are the things they put you people through."

"Keep moving," Ardo said. "Just through to the other side."

"What's wrong? Are you all right?"

"Just keep moving," Ardo snapped.

"You don't like this place, do you? You're frightened of it. I can feel it."

"Lady, I said *move!*"

Merdith winced at the shout and quickly walked to the opposite door.

"Go right," Ardo ordered. He felt slightly dizzy. He loved resoc . . . he hated resoc . . . he looked forward to resoc . . . he would rather shoot himself than do resoc again.

Merdith quickly opened the door and stepped off into the brightly lit corridor beyond, with Ardo too closely on her heels. They moved past the barracks cells proper, including the one where Ardo had stowed his gear earlier, and passed through the final doorway to the galley.

It was a cramped but efficient room. Whatever had happened to take the personnel of the base away had apparently not been during anyone's regular dining shift. The compartment was pristine. Ardo was just as glad that no one had left anything behind. He was weary of the constant reminders that the place had been so fully occupied hours ago and was now so completely desolate.

"Nice place you have here," Merdith observed casually. "Sterile, but nice."

"The food dispensers are back along that wall," Ardo said, motioning with the rifle again. "They're not hard to operate. Just—"

"I know my way around a kitchen, soldier-boy." Merdith stepped toward the bank of meal and drink dispensers. "You want anything? Cup of coffee?"

"No, ma'am. Don't drink coffee."

Merdith pulled a cup from the dispenser and began filling it. "Really? That's interesting. Did you know that coffee was one of the things most people begged to have sent with them when the original colonies were exiled from Earth?"

"Yes, ma'am, I'd heard that."

Merdith turned around with her steaming cup and leaned back against the wall. Silence fell between them. There was so much that Ardo wanted to ask, but the questions tumbled through his mind, running into each other. What was she saying before Littlefield came in? Something about it all being a lie? But now that he thought about it, he couldn't recall what they had been talking about exactly.

"So, we gonna be disturbed anytime soon?"

Ardo came back from his thoughts, realizing angrily that letting himself drift away like that while guarding this woman might well get him killed. "Sorry? What, ma'am?"

"Are we alone? Anyone gonna be bothering us for a while?"

Ardo flushed. "Please, ma'am, I really don't think you ought to be talking that way. It isn't . . . isn't right."

Merdith started to answer but stopped. Her slack mouth quickly became a delighted smile. "You thought I wanted to—"

"Now, ma'am, it doesn't matter what I thought." Ardo could feel his face going beet red and knew there was not a thing he could do to stop it. "I'm . . . I'm guarding you and it wouldn't be proper."

"Proper?" Merdith was having entirely too much fun and Ardo knew it was at his expense.

"Yes, ma'am! Proper!"

"I don't believe it." Merdith took a long sip of her coffee and then tipped it in salute toward Ardo. "You're a virgin."

Ardo knew his voice was too loud when he opened his mouth. "I don't see that it's any of your business, ma'am!"

"Now I *know* I've seen everything!" Merdith was delighted. "A virgin Confederacy Marine!"

"It wouldn't be honorable, ma'am . . . not to either one of us. Now, why don't you just sip your coffee and relax . . . I mean . . . we've got an hour before you're due back . . ." The more he talked, the worse it seemed to get. Finally Ardo just let his words trail off into a frustrated silence.

Merdith looked away, amusement still in her eyes. "Don't worry, soldier-boy, your secret is safe with me." She sat down smoothly at one of the tables. "Besides, that really isn't what I meant. You're a nice guy and all, soldier-boy, but all I honestly want to do is talk. That is what you had in mind, isn't it?"

"Yes, ma'am. I—"

"Call me Merdith."

"Oh, I don't know if I—"

"Sure, it's just us. Let's be friends."

"Okay . . . Merdith. I'm . . . I'm PFC Ardo Melnikov."

The woman tipped her cup again in thanks. "Okay, Ardo. It's nice to meet you. So . . . tell me. How is it that you fine Marines came to rescue my sorry soul?"

Ardo thought for a moment. "I'm sorry, ma'am, I can't discuss mission details with—"

"With a civilian, I know," Merdith finished the sentence for him. "I'm just curious about how you got me out of there. The last few days are a bit hazy for me. Where did you find me?"

"Oh, I didn't find you, ma'am. That was Cutter— PFC Koura-Abi. That big guy you met earlier in Ops."

"Of course. So where did *he* find me?"

"Don't really know, ma'am. First thing I saw he had you over his shoulder and was running back to join the rest of us at the barricade."

Merdith's eyes smiled warmly at him. "I see. So how did we get out of there? The lieutenant mentioned something about her 'evac' deserting her?"

"Oh," Ardo shrugged. "There was a Dropship with us that was supposed to extract us when we had that box. We fought our way to the extraction landing zone, but . . . it never showed up."

"I thought you said it was with you?"

"Yeah. Strange, that. I heard it talking about its final approach to the landing zone—it's all on the com channel—but we never saw it. It just—I don't know— wasn't there. The Zerg had cut off our retreat and it looked like it was time for us all to cash our last paycheck. The lieutenant, though, she had us fight our way out of there. We lost a few along the way, but what's left of us are still here. If the Dropship had come, we'd have been okay. Some sort of SNAFU, I guess."

"A SNAFU?" Merdith nodded absently with a slight smile playing on the edge of her lips. "Yeah, I guess it could be that, although your lieutenant seems to have more than her share of them. What was all that about a nuke?"

"Oh, that," Ardo shrugged again, but his face settled into an uncertain frown. "Well, after we hightailed it across the Basin, the Confederacy nuked Oasis. Just a little tactical. Good thing, too, or those Zerg would have followed us and taken us all out at the wall."

"Well, we wouldn't have wanted that," Merdith sighed, but her brows were knit together in deep and troubled thought. She came to a conclusion, her brow smoothing as she looked up again with a quickly flashed smile at Ardo. "Well, we made it thanks to you—me to my life of thermal wells and you to thoughts of that girl of yours. What was her name? Oh, yeah, Melani."

Ardo swallowed. "What do you know about Melani? You said she was a lie, or something was a lie. What were you talking about?"

Merdith gazed down into her coffee. She looked for all the world to Ardo as though she were reading the swirls like some kind of gypsy divination rite.

"The truth is dangerous, Ardo. You're a nice little soldier-boy. Maybe it's better not to discuss these things."

Ardo put his boot on the bench opposite where Merdith was sitting and leaned forward. "Ma'am—

Merdith—a wise man once told me that truth is the only thing that is real. Truth is what's left when all the shadows and darkness are torn away. I believe that and I think you do, too."

"What I believe isn't the point here," Merdith replied, looking at Ardo as if for the first time. "The point is what you believe."

Ardo did not understand what she was saying. All he knew is that he wanted to know the truth, that he was tired of the shadows haunting his mind and driving him slowly mad. "What happened to Melani? What happened to my parents? What happened to my world?"

Merdith sighed. "Ardo . . . You remember we were talking about Pandora's box?"

"What?" Was she changing the subject on him? "Yeah, we were talking about the metal case we found with you . . ."

"Yes, that's true, but I'm asking if you remember the story?"

"Sure I do. What's the point?"

"You've got a Pandora's box inside you. Do you really want me to open it? Once it's open, you can never, ever close it up again."

Ardo winced. His head was beginning to pound once more. "You're saying the answer is inside of me?"

Merdith seemed to come to a decision. "Tell me about that last day. Tell me everything about that last day with Melani on your old home world."

The pounding in his skull increased. "What does that have to do with—"

"Just tell me," Merdith insisted. "Start at the beginning of where things went wrong—you know there was a moment when things just started to go wrong—what were you doing just before that?"

Ardo winced against the pain. Why was she making him do this? Why was he allowing himself to do this? He didn't know this woman. She was probably a spy or anarchist or God knew what.

He had to know. He had to know the truth.

"We . . . we were in a field . . ."

Golden . . . a perfect day that comes along all too rarely . . .

" . . . having a picnic. It was the most beautiful day. Warm in the spring. Oh, God . . . do I have to . . ."

"It's all right," Merdith assured him. "I'm here with you. We'll walk through the day together and I'll be there with you. What changed that perfect day?"

"The siren in the township went off. The alarm siren. I thought it was the usual noonday test, but Melani said it wasn't noon and then . . . they came."

"Who came?"

The sun was dowsed in that instant. Enormous plumes of smoke trailed behind fireballs roaring directly toward him from the western end of the broad valley.

"The Zerg came."

"Can you see them? What do they look like?"

"I can't see them . . . just balls of fire coming down through the atmosphere."

"What kind of entry would cause that, Ardo?"

Ardo blinked. "What do you mean?"

"What would cause the Zerg to make big fireballs and smoke contrails in the sky like that?" Merdith pressed. Her eyes were locked on his as she spoke.

"High speed, I guess. A lot of heat builds up on atmospheric entry, I suppose," Ardo replied.

"But have you *ever* heard of the Zerg entering a planetary atmosphere that way?" Merdith asked softly. "They swarm across space. Their arrival is soft and silent."

Ardo closed his eyes. The light in the room seemed to be hurting them. "What . . . what are you saying?"

"*I'm* not saying anything. I'm *listening*," Merdith said. "Just try to relax and remember. Talk to me. Please . . . what did you and Melani do next?"

"Well . . . we ran! We ran toward the township. The old colony had a defensive wall and we thought we might be safer inside. I don't know how we got there, but the next thing I remember was that we were inside along with everyone else."

The rattle of automatic weapons clattered suddenly from the perimeter wall. Two dull explosive thuds resounded, followed by even more chattering machine guns.

"What was it like?" Merdith urged quietly, her eyes fixed on Ardo as she sipped her coffee.

"Well . . . chaos! The Zerg were attacking and—"

"No, I mean, tell me what you *saw*. Tell me what you *did*."

Ardo closed his eyes.

"Please, Ardo!" Melani said. "I . . . Where do we go? What do we do?"

Ardo glanced around. He could taste the panic in the air.

"We were in the square. It's a large open area in the middle of the town. We used to have concerts there or plays in the summer evenings. I'd never seen it so crowded. We were shoulder to shoulder. Melani . . . I held her hand and we tried to cross the square."

"Yes, that's right." Merdith put the cup down. Her unblinking eyes remained fixed on Ardo. "What did you see next?"

Ardo felt suddenly cold. His eyes shut against the images that came unbidden from the depths of his mind.

A sheet of flame erupted beyond the fortress's outer wall. Its crimson light flashed against the blanket of smoke that hung oppressively over the town. The blood-red hue fell across the panicked crowd in the square. Screams, shouts, and cries all tumbled into a cacophony of sound, but several disembodied voices penetrated Ardo's thoughts clearly.

"It's the Confederacy forces! It's the Marines!"

"No!" Ardo reeled backward from the table, his combat suit slamming into the wall behind him. The plastic wall cracked under the sudden impact. "That's not what he said!"

"What *did* he say, Ardo?" Merdith was standing now, leaning forward, both her hands on the table. "What did you *hear*?"

"He said . . . he must have said . . . *'Where . . . where are the Confederacy—'* "

"That's a lie, Ardo!" Merdith shot back. "Remember! Think! Neural resocialization can't replace memories; it can only cover them over with new ones! What did you *hear?*"

"Ardo, I'm frightened!" Melani's eyes were wide and liquid. "What is it? What's going on?"

There were so many words he wanted to say to her in that moment—so many words that he would regret never having said for uncounted years to come.

"Tell me what you *see!*" Merdith demanded.

The eastern wall had been breached. The old rampart was being pulled down from the other side, dismantled before Ardo's eyes. It seemed as though a dark wave was breaking against the breach.

"Stop it!" Ardo screamed. "What are you doing to me?"

"You wanted the truth. You've opened the truth, in yourself," Merdith said. "The ugly, horrible truth and it won't go back in the box, Ardo. Not again. What did you *see*, Ardo? What happened next, Ardo?"

Ardo slid along the wall toward the door of the mess room, reeling backward away from Merdith. He wanted to run, wanted to get as far from this woman as possible, but somewhere in his mind he knew that he was not trying to run from her but from the beast lurking in his own mind.

Ardo heard Melani gasp behind him. "I can't . . . I can't breathe . . ."

The mob was crushing them. Ardo looked desperately around him, trying to find a way out.

Movement overhead caught his eye. The angular, bloated form of a Confederacy Dropship, still glowing from the fast atmospheric interface of landing, was dropping down overhead.

Tears flooded Ardo's eyes.

Tears flooded Ardo's eyes.

The downblast from the engines created an instant hurricane in the panicked crowd. Ardo blinked through the dust as the Dropship lowered its transport ramp into the square. He could see the silhouetted figures of Confederacy Marines . . .

They grabbed him.

They tore him from Melani's hand.

"Melani!" he screamed.

"Melani!" Ardo screamed in the mess hall.

"Please, Ardo! Don't leave me alone!" she cried as the Marines dragged him into their ship.

Ardo struggled to escape them as the ramp closed. Something hit him from behind and his world went black . . .

Slowly, the world grew brighter. Ardo was sitting on the floor. His eyes focused slowly on Merdith. She knelt beside him, her hand on his tear-streaked cheek.

Her voice was heavy with emotion. "Poor soldier-boy. It's been that way all over the colony worlds, from what we hear. The Confederacy needs to build an army as fast as they can. They've been press-ganging boys for over a year now and then using their neural resocialization to layer as many false memories on top of their existing ones as necessary—until their manufactured soldier-boys believe whatever the Confederacy *needs* them to believe. They go where they are told to go. They die when they are told to die."

"Then Melani . . . my folks . . ." Ardo struggled for breath.

"I don't know, Ardo, but they almost certainly didn't die the way you remember it happening, and most likely didn't die at all."

"Then everything I know is a lie," Ardo said weakly.

"Perhaps," Merdith said. "But if you're willing to help me, I think we both may be able to get off this cursed world. I can help you if—"

Ardo pressed the muzzle of his rifle firmly under Merdith's chin.

CHAPTER 16

BARRICADES

"WHAT HAVE YOU DONE TO ME?" ARDO SHUD-dered, his hand quivering on the trigger of the C-14 assault rifle.

Merdith held very still. Her voice was quiet and terribly deliberate as she spoke. "Not a thing, Ardo. Not one blessed thing."

"Get back!" Ardo could hardly see beyond the pain banging against the back of his forehead. He was having trouble focusing. "Just back off slowly."

"I'm so sorry, soldier-boy."

"Don't touch me!" Ardo squealed, his voice shaking with terror and outrage. The gun muzzle shivered under Merdith's chin.

Merdith slowly raised both her hands, palms open toward the Marine. "Okay Ardo. I'm going to back away now. Just relax."

Merdith rose up with aching slowness, smoothly backing against the mess hall table. Her eyes were locked with Ardo's, unblinking and holding his attention.

Ardo steadied his rifle but found its aim wandering dangerously. He could not seem to keep it steady. He wanted to stand, to get some distance between himself and the woman sliding slowly back to sit on the table.

She had done something to him, something to his mind. It was a trick, some sort of drug or attack that he had not seen. He tried to remember the way it had been—that perfect, golden day turning blood red. He could see the Zerg pouring through the breach in the town wall, and he could see the Confederacy Marines doing the same thing. The Zerg were tearing at Melani and the Marines were dragging her away all at the same time and in the same place. He had two truths in his head at the same time. He knew that they could not both be true, but that knowledge did not help him choose between them. He longed for sleep, some blessed place of unconsciousness where he could awake from this nightmare and his thoughts would have all been sorted out for him.

Both memories could not be real, but inside himself he realized that somehow they both *were* real and that the full truth lay beyond both memories. He dreaded the answer, either way, but he also knew that he had to have it, whatever the cost. Something within him demanded the truth.

Ardo staggered to his feet, regaining his composure

as best he could. He breathed deeply to calm himself. His rifle aim steadied.

Merdith made no move, no sound.

"What did you do to me?" Ardo asked levelly.

"*I* didn't do anything to you," she replied calmly. "You might ask that same question of the Confederacy—"

"Cut the crap, lady," Ardo snapped. "I may not be playing the same game you are, but that doesn't mean I can't read the score. You did something to my head"—Ardo jammed the rifle muzzle toward her head for emphasis—"so what did you do to me?"

"I didn't plant anything in your mind, if that's what you mean."

Ardo raised the rifle to his shoulder, squaring his aim between her eyes.

"Easy!" Merdith leaned back slightly, her arms still raised. "I swear. All I did is . . . unkink what was already there. Look, I'm a psych, okay? I'm an unregistered psych. I fell through the screening process—it happens sometimes in the outer colonies. They never suspected. I wasn't interested in the Confederacy psych program, so I just kept quiet about it. I'm not trained or anything—I just have a gift for helping people get their minds straightened out sometimes, that's all. I swear, that's all."

Ardo lowered the weapon slightly. He considered her words for a moment before he spoke again. "Tell me: what *really* happened to my family? What happened to Melani?"

"I don't know."

Ardo brought the weapon up quickly again.

"I don't know!" Panic, anger and frustration tumbled through Merdith's voice, her words rushing in staccato sounds as she spoke. "I don't know! Maybe they're alive! Maybe not! How should I know? They're your memories, not mine!"

"Aahh!" Ardo grunted as he lowered his weapon in disgust. "Worthless! You're absolutely worthless!"

"Look, soldier-boy, I didn't do this to you," she answered. "Neural resocialization just layers new memories on top of old ones—it doesn't replace them. All I did was help you straighten out your head a little."

Ardo shook his head. "But you still can't tell me which memory is the real one and which is the false one, can you?"

"You were the one who wanted to know the truth," she said sullenly.

"Yeah? What truth?" Ardo growled. "*Which* truth?"

"I don't *know* which truth. But you *do* want to know what the truth really is, don't you?"

Ardo look at her and considered. She had opened his mind. There was no closing Pandora's box now. "Yes . . . I have to know!"

She sighed through a slight smile. "Then help me and I'll help you find that truth. I know some people who can get us off this world. Help me get in touch with them . . . reach them . . . and they'll help us, too. We'll go back to your planet . . . uh . . . ."

"Bountiful," he finished for her quietly. The word was almost too painfully beautiful to say.

"Yes, back to Bountiful. And we'll find the truth together."

Ardo was about to answer her when the com channel chimed in his ear. He responded automatically. "Melnikov here."

"Escort the prisoner to Operations on the double, Private." Littlefield's voice sounded somehow different to Ardo, but the private had enough worries of his own to think about it much.

"By your word, sir," Ardo responded, then turned to Merdith. "That's enough coffee and conversation. Let's go."

The lift had not even cleared the Level 3 landing before Ardo could hear the voices yelling overhead.

". . . supposed to do once we storm the transport? You've heard the tactical channel traffic. Do *you* have a better option?"

"I don't know! I don't have all the answers! All I know is that I'm not giving up on these grunts, Breanne! They deserve better than this!"

"Yes, they do, and that's exactly my point. If we'd been good little soldiers we would have sat under that *nuke* and caught the damn thing with our teeth. That's what they wanted, isn't it? But we're here and still breathing."

"So just what the hell are you telling me, ma'am?"

"I'm saying I don't like this any more than you do,

Littlefield, but we are running out of options! You have a better idea, then fine! Let's hear it right now!"

The lift seemed agonizingly slow. Ardo glanced at Merdith. Her face was a blank, but Ardo could see that her eyes were focused and intent. She was soaking in every word drifting down from above.

"I don't *have* an answer!" Littlefield rumbled. "Someone must have screwed up! If we just get on the tactical channel, we can get this thing straightened out with CHQ!"

The lift cleared the floor plates of the Operations Room. Breanne was standing on the island, her arms folded defiantly across her chest as she leaned back against one of the consoles, staring down at the map table. Littlefield's face was ruddy as he faced her, his large fists gripping the edge of the map table. His knuckles were nearly white with fury. Between them stood Tinker Jans at the far side of the island. He looked to Ardo as though he were caught in a crossfire and trying to make himself as small and as still as possible.

"Look for yourself! That's satellite data, Sergeant. Clean band and updated in real time." Breanne's finger stabbed out suddenly, indicating each location as she spoke. "Zerg infestations moving in from the northeast in a ragged line here, here, and here. Advanced recon groups will be reaching those outer settlements in the next few minutes. The rest of the northeast settlements will be hit within an hour after that. Where are our Marines on this map, Sergeant?"

Littlefield stared at the map and said nothing.

"They're all at Mar Sara Starport," Breanne answered for him. "Confederacy Dropships have been evac'ing every position for the last three hours. All of the heavy equipment is gone. There are still ground forces being brought to the central transports at Mar Sara Starport, but those will be loaded within the hour. Dropships are returning from the outposts now with the last remaining Marines. Tinker's brother, the esteemed Tegis Marz, is returning from his last run now."

"The same guy that left us high and dry last time?" Littlefield was incredulous. "What makes you think that he'll go out of his way to come back for us now?"

"Because we aren't the ones who are going to do the asking," Breanne replied, her eyes flashing. "Tegis has been choking the com channels for the last half hour trying to find out who brought his brother out of our little garrison here. Apparently he doesn't know his brother got left behind."

"Hey, it wasn't my fault!" Tinker said. "I went out to repair the downlink. Who knew the SCV was balky. It quit on me out there and I had to hoof it back. I ran like hell when I saw the Dropships hovering over the base, but by the time I got back they were gone."

"I'm glad you did." The lieutenant's smile was wicked. "You're my new best friend, Tinker. You'll call your brother once he's on the ground over the com channel and convince him to come and get you." She looked up at Littlefield. "When Tegis comes to get his brother, we rush the ship and take it back to the Starport. Then we'll straighten out this SNAFU and get the hell off this planet."

"You can't do that!" Merdith interrupted.

"Ah, Ms. Jernic." Breanne noticed Ardo and his prisoner for the first time since they arrived. "It seems you'll be joining us on a little trip."

Merdith ignored the remark. "Without the Confederacy outposts, there will be nothing left to stop the Zerg!"

Breanne shrugged. "Well, there's always the vaunted local militia . . ."

"They don't have either the equipment or the numbers to stop a planetary infestation!" Merdith started to walk toward the command island, but Ardo grabbed her arm, firmly restraining her. "What about the civilians? What about *their* evacuation?"

"The Confederacy," Breanne grumbled, "has apparently written off the planet . . . including its civilians."

Merdith struggled against Ardo's grip, but the Marine held her back. "Written us off to the Zerg? It was that Confederacy device that *brought* the Zerg here! With all their weapons and all their starships and all their soldier-boy Marines, they wanted more power. So they built that box, not even comprehending the death it would bring with it. They thought they could control them or capture them. They had no idea what they had unleashed. And now they're just 'writing us off' as though we were some cipher on a balance sheet!"

No one in the room had an answer for her.

Merdith stopped struggling, anger still in her face.

"A planet full of monsters. I just thought I'd never see them among my own kind."

Breanne looked up, her wicked smile returning under the bristle of her hair. "You never know, do you?"

"Lieutenant," Littlefield interrupted. "Tac-com one-twenty-nine."

"On speakers," Breanne commanded.

"This is the Vixen *on radial three-four-zero, forty-five clicks to MS Station . . . stand by to refuel for immediate dustoff."*

"Negative, Vixen. *Report to the OOD for evac on landing."*

"Hey, he'll be on the ground there inside of ten minutes," Tinker said nervously. "Maybe . . . maybe they won't let him leave again once he's on the ground."

"Any word on my request regarding Scenic Station?"

Ardo looked up at the speakers.

"Negative. No contact."

"What about that personnel request? I gotta find that tech!"

"CHQ has no information for you at this time."

"All right, you know the drill," Breanne said. "Jans, get on the horn and call—"

"*Lieutenant, this is Xiang! We have multiple contacts bearing oh-five-five degrees!*"

Breanne glanced down at the map table, her eyes suddenly wide. "Where? How many?"

"*There's a . . . Stand by . . . There's about twenty . . . maybe twenty-five passing to the south. Hydralisks, I think, ma'am. And . . . oh, hell! There's a flight of eight Mutalisks above them.*"

"They're not on the map," Breanne seethed. "Why aren't they on the map?"

"*The Mutalisks are turning. They are vectoring toward the base. Permission to fire, ma'am?*"

Breanne continued to stare angrily at the map table.

"*Permission to fire, ma'am?*"

All of the color drained from Tinker's face.

Littlefield looked up. "Breanne?"

The lieutenant shook herself from her frozen state. "Negative! Hold your fire!"

"What . . . what do you mean, hold your fire?" The technician's eyes darted around in fear.

"Listen to me! We don't want this fight right now." Breanne motioned everyone else up to the command island. "Everyone take cover! If anyone is spotted, open fire, but until then stay out of site. Don't transmit, just monitor. There have been reports that the Zerg can follow transmissions to their source. Just wait for my command, and hope like hell they pass us by!"

"What is the universe coming to," Littlefield muttered, "when Marines start hiding under desks!"

Ardo propelled Merdith up the short ladder to the command island. As he did, light blossomed to the west. Through the windows he saw in the east the glowing trail of the first Confederacy evac ship arching into the sky.

CHAPTER 17

WEAK LINKS

ARDO VAULTED UP THE LADDER TO THE COM-
mand island. The space was crowded enough with the
large equipment banks nearly completely surrounding
the map table in the center. The combat suit only
made things worse in the cramped space. Still, the
consoles were built to Marine specs and designed for
durability as much as for functionality. They had a
clear path to the lift. Ardo wondered why they did not
all just disappear into the bowels of the Command
Center rather than try to duck for cover behind the
consoles of a fish bowl like Operations.

Breanne crouched behind the map table. It was not
the first time Ardo was struck with her catlike movement. She switched off the display on the map table,
then smoothly pulled a large set of field binoculars up
to her eyes. "Six of them . . . no, make that seven.
Mutalisks flying cover for a ground force of . . . let's
see . . . maybe fifteen or twenty Hydralisks about a
half mile to the south." Breanne slid back down next

to the table, out of sight of the windows. "There may be more beyond that, maybe a mile or two. It's difficult to say. The main force seems to be passing us by. Everyone stay put. Let the flyers have their fun ogling the 'old abandoned human base.' Once they're a few clicks safely away from here we'll make the call and catch our ride home."

Ardo sat with his back against a console directly opposite to Jans. The engineer was intent on every word Breanne was saying. He was pale even in the dim light of the Operations Room and nodded rather more vehemently than he probably should have. Jans swallowed hard, then his head slowly turned toward the ladder exit from the island just to his left. Ardo followed the man's gaze. He was staring toward the tactical communication panel just below the catwalk to the west. It was still lit, the muted words of the chatter of the starport still pouring out of it through the speakers mounted above the island.

"*Transit alpha four-oh-niner, cleared for immediate departure pad seven. Transit alpha oh-six-five hold short at pad fourteen. Transit gamma eight-zero-zero cleared to pad twelve. Transit delta two-two-zero, hold at Lima for cross traffic . . .*"

Jans's eyes grew large as a second flare of light erupted through the western windows above the taccom console. "There goes another one," he breathed.

"They aren't wasting any time getting out," Littlefield muttered. The sergeant seemed distracted and detached, his mind working on a different problem.

Ardo knew it was his imagination, but the knowledge did not help him. The chatter from the speakers seemed unbearably loud. "Shouldn't we shut that off?"

Breanne shook her head, looking up as she listened. "Too late. They're here."

Ardo realized he could hear it, too: the fingernails-on-slate sound of the Mutalisks screaming at each other as they neared the human base. The sound cut through the windows to reach their ears, mixing with the constant chatter from the tac-com open channel.

"*Transit alpha oh-six-five cleared for immediate departure pad fourteen . . .*"

"*Control.* Vixen *inbound requesting vector . . .*"

Jans caught his breath.

"Vixen, *hold at nav marker Ta-shua and stand by; the pattern is full.*"

"*Roger, control, holding at Ta-shua.*"

Another column of flame and smoke tore upward through the darkening atmosphere.

Merdith crouched next to Ardo, hugging her knees to her chest. "Looks like you soldier-boys are going to miss your boat."

Breanne's eyes reflected a practiced indifference. "We're not finished yet, Ms. Jernic."

"No, of course not," Merdith responded evenly. "All I'm saying is that if you *did* happen to miss your boat, you might want to consider other means of departure."

"Ah," Breanne smiled back at her, baring her teeth, "you mean throw our lot in with a spy and a traitor, perhaps?"

"Sorry to disappoint you, Lieutenant," Merdith shrugged, "but I'm no spy."

"No, of course not." Breanne casually looked away toward the windows. "Not a spy, not a collaborator, not an expert doing weapons research for the Sons of Korhal. You are just an innocent civilian engineer who was found in accidental possession of a highly classified piece of Confederacy equipment." Breanne stopped, turned to Merdith and smiled frostily. "Look, Ms. Jernic, I choose to believe you. I choose to believe you because if I choose otherwise I'll have Mister Melnikov here take you out of this Command Center and shoot you as many times as necessary to insure that you are very permanently dead. Now, you don't want me to choose *not* to believe that, do you?"

Merdith considered the angular face in front of her carefully. "No, Lieutenant, I most certainly do not."

"Then, Ms. Jernic"—Breanne sniffed derisively—"for the time being, you keep your company and I'll keep mine."

"Whatever you say, Lieutenant," Merdith spoke casually. "However, may I point out that *your* friends are apparently leaving the planet in droves while *my* friends may soon be the only ones with a ticket off this planet. Even if you *do* manage to get back to the starport somehow, just how pleased will your superiors be to see you? Nobody likes to see a dead man walking in the door . . . especially when it's in everyone's best interest that the body *stay* dead."

A horrible scraping sound rang through the tritanium roof of the Operations Room. Ardo winced against the sound, pulling his rifle up closer to his chest in his sudden tension.

"Hold still." Breanne breathed out her words as quietly as she could manage. "They're here."

Everyone looked up. The sound of scraping scales on serrated tails dragged casually across the armor shivered through the plates overhead. The sound occasionally obliterated the surreal voices so casually communicating from the still operating tac-com transceiver.

"Transit gamma eight-zero-zero, cleared to depart pad twelve immediately. Transit epsilon four-three-three, hold short at rho-beta intersection."

There were two additional scraping impacts on the roof plates. Ardo could clearly hear the dreadful, screeching voices of the Mutalisks as they slithered about the rooftop. He glanced at Jans across from him. The man was sweating profusely, his eyes fixed on the transceiver as though somehow he could crawl through the device and somehow join the distant voice on the other side.

"Transit epsilon four-three-three clear to proceed to pad ten . . ."

"Control, this is Vixen *holding at Ta-shua. What's the delay? I've got to see the base commander and . . ."*

"Vixen, you are cleared to land. Report at outer marker. Over."

"What about my brother? I don't know . . ."

Jans gritted his teeth. Another voice came across the com channel, not nearly so detached.

"Marz, for the last time, he's probably already off-planet in an unreported transport. Get your ass down out of the sky right now."

"Copy that, sir! Vixen *on final appr . . . repor . . . outer mark . . ."*

Ardo glanced at Littlefield, whispering. "The transmission's breaking up?"

"The Mutalisks," Littlefield sighed. "They're playing with the antenna dishes."

" . . . final appr . . . tand by."

" . . . oger . . . ansit epsilon four-three . . . eared for . . . mediate departure pad seven-left. Vixen, *taxi left to platform seven-three for shutdown."*

"Roger, control. Vixen *taxiing to platform seven-three."*

Breanne pointed to her ear and then toward the ceiling. Ardo strained to hear.

The scraping sound had stopped.

Littlefield put his thumbs together and moved his hands like flapping wings. Breanne shrugged and shook her head, her eyebrows knitted together in doubt.

Ardo unconsciously held his breath. He was concentrating so hard on the sounds overhead that he did not notice Merdith's nudge until her second try.

She was pointing toward Tinker Jans.

Ardo could see at once that the man was in bad shape. His pale skin glistened with sweat. He was physically shaking, his lips moving as he spoke to himself. His eyes were fixed on the transmission console just a few steps from the base of the command island.

"Transit kappa oh-seven-five cleared for immediate departure. Vixen, what is your status?"

"Are they gone?" Littlefield hissed.

Breanne shook her head. She did not know.

"My load has disembarked, control. I'm clean."

"Roger, Vixen. Shut down and proceed to platform five-right. Report to the section chief there for embarkation and departure."

"No!" Jans whimpered. "Don't leave me here!"

"Don't leave me alone!" Melani wept. Ardo froze.

"Vixen, roger that. Shutting down . . ."

"No!"

Jans hauled himself up in a single movement. Ardo lunged for him, but he was too late. The engineer propelled himself through the gap between the consoles of the command island, running across the floor plates.

"Quick! Stop him!" Breanne snapped.

Ardo sprang to his feet, clearing the access ladder in a jump, but he could not reach the engineer.

Tinker Jans swept up the dangling communications microphone and keyed the transmit button.

"Tegis! It's Jans! I'm here! Don't leave me! I'm back at the base at Scenic! They left me behind, they—"

Ardo had no time to think as he ran across the floor. When he reached Jans, he simply drew back his combat suit fist and launched it at the engineer's head.

The power-enhanced, armored glove did its job well. Jans fell unconscious to the floor.

"Jans! Jans! I'm coming to get you! Just hold on and . . . hey! Let go of me! That's my brother out there! You can't—"

Shattering windows drowned the words out. The transparent panes exploded into the room. Instinctively, Ardo ducked away from the cascading crystal. He heard the sudden chattering of automatic fire in the room.

Above the screeching, Ardo heard Breanne's unmistakable voice filling the com channel. "Open fire! Open fire and kill them all!"

CHAPTER 18

JAWS OF VICTORY

ARDO DOVE BACK TOWARD THE COMMAND IS-
land, instinctively arming his rifle. He was still rolling
upright when he began discharging his weapon.

Three Mutalisks launched themselves through the
framework of the shattered windows. Their purplish
wings were shredded on the remaining shards, but
the creatures were oblivious to the damage they were
inflicting on themselves. There was madness in their
flat, blood-brown eyes: mindless, relentless, and deadly.
Ear-piercing screams erupted from their wide, gaping
mouths as they charged.

"Keep firing! Keep firing!" Breanne shouted
through the com channel. Ardo was happy to oblige.
His gauss rifle joined the hail of death erupting from
the guns on the command island just behind him.

Wing membrane, cartilage, skin, muscle, all exploded in shreds from the ugly beasts as they fanati-
cally moved forward. The wet pieces slammed against
the panels, ceiling, and floor, exploding into acrid

smoke. Within seconds the entire command chamber was filled with the swirling, thick stench that even the outside wind, now howling through the shattered windows, could not dissipate.

Ardo continued to press his fire. He could see the nearest Mutalisk open its mouth, its jaw muscles working. He had a glimpse of fanglike projections on either side of its massive jaw.

It's attacking, Ardo suddenly realized. He dove to his left.

A gush of bat-winged abominations disgorged from the creature's maw toward the base of the command island where Ardo had just squatted. The sightless creatures splayed against the metal, erupting on impact. The floor plates melted away in a terrible, high-pitched squeal. The Mutalisk shifted the fowl stream, attempting to follow Ardo, but the Marine was too quick for the creature. His feet under him, he sprang forward toward the alcove of the elevator door.

The deadly eruption continued to follow him, the Mutalisk now fixed on Ardo as its only thought. The vomited creatures slammed in a line across the floor, the plates dissolving like water under their impact. Acrid smoke filled the room, making it difficult for Ardo to breathe with his faceplate still up. He scrambled toward the elevator alcove. The curved door was closed. To the left and right of the elevator were the raised platforms above the control stations.

There was no other cover. He was running out of places to hide.

He reached the elevator bay and slammed his hand against the call button. He turned quickly, his open palm repeatedly smashing down on the button. He glimpsed the hellish rush of winged abominations issue from the Mutalisk's maw, evaporating metal in a straight line toward him.

Suddenly the Mutalisk's horrible attack stopped. Ardo looked up. The head of the Mutalisk exploded under a stream of tracer fire from the command island. Bits of the creature rained down around the room. Several greasy pieces impacted on Ardo's battle armor, the creature's latent acid clawing at the metal fabric of the suit. Ardo yelled incoherently as he brushed the pieces away quickly with his gloved hands. His suit was badly pocked, but he did not think anything had burned all the way through.

His pursuer fell heavily to the floor, the impact almost immediately dissolving the plates beneath him. A gaping, smoking hole was all that was left of the place where the creature fell as it burned down through the deck. By the sounds coming from the fissure, it was still burning its way down through several decks of the Command Center.

Ardo, his back to the elevator door, raised his weapon again. He searched desperately through the smoke swirling madly about the room, but he had lost sight of his companions. For that matter, he suddenly realized, the weapons from the command island had gone silent.

"Lieutenant?" Ardo asked tentatively.

Overhead, Ardo could still hear the tac-com channel. " . . . *Repeat,* Vixen, *return to base at once. That is a direct order!*"

"*Jans! Hold on! Tegis is on the way! I'm comin' for ya, kid!*"

Marz! Ardo realized. He must have gotten the message! He was inbound right now. All they had to do was . . .

Ardo swallowed. All they had to do was be here.

The rotating emergency lights flashed through the swirling, acrid smoke. Jans might just be his ticket out of here, he suddenly realized. If everyone on the command island were dead, then he could pull Jans out to the Dropship. He could tell Tegis that he had been left behind, too. What the hell did he care about the mission or that damn box! If he could get off-world then maybe he could find a way out of the resoc tanks and make his way back to Bountiful. Maybe he could get his life back all over again and to hell with the Marines and their Confederacy! Then, maybe he could find out if his life had been a lie. Maybe, just maybe, Melani was still there somewhere, looking for him, waiting for him. Maybe, just maybe . . .

Ardo shouldered his weapon. The smoke was still thick in the room, but Ardo remembered where Jans had fallen. He quickly began picking his way across the gaping rifts in the floor. Jans had fallen somewhere near the transmitter console to the left of the command island. If he could just get there before anyone noticed him, he could sip out AWOL in the confusion and then use Jans to get off this rock. He could quit this damn Confederacy and its Marines and get back his life.

The Marine moved with a wary anticipation. There were still at least two more Mutalisks out there somewhere. Maybe they were dead but more likely they were lurking nearby.

"Scenic Base, this is the Vixen *five miles out from the marker! Jans, please respond! Jans! Please respond . . ."*

Ardo reached Jans. The tech was still out cold where Ardo had decked him.

Something struck the side of his combat helmet. Ardo did not notice it at first, but it was followed by a second light impact.

Ardo quickly grabbed his weapon and swiveled toward the command island. Heart suddenly racing, he saw Lieutenant Breanne through the swirling smoke, crouching next to the map table. Merdith was just behind her. Littlefield crouched on the other side of the map table.

Breanne signaled for Ardo to hold his position. She then pointed her first two fingers toward her own eyes and then pointed at Ardo.

Ardo understood the standard signal and looked once more around the compartment. The smoke was quickly clearing from the room. Acid had clearly damaged many of the consoles, and there were several melted troughs in the room. Smoke still poured from the hole burned by the fallen Mutalisk, but otherwise the room appeared clear. Ardo looked back at Breanne and shook his head.

Breanne nodded a curt acknowledgment and then pointed down at the technician.

Ardo looked down quickly. There was a nasty bruise coloring a rather large knob rising on the side of his head. He certainly didn't envy the man the headache he'd have later . . . if he woke up. Ardo realized with a start that he did not actually care if the man ever woke up, as long as he could use him to get on that Dropship.

Ardo looked back at Breanne and held out his hand palm down and level. Stable, he signaled.

Again, Breanne nodded. She pointed at Jans, then at Ardo, and then signaled the Marine toward the elevator.

He had forgotten about the elevator! Ardo glanced behind him. The curved door had rolled back and the elevator itself now stood open and ready for them. He nodded again toward Breanne. He reached down and grabbed the unconscious technician by the collar of his fatigue jacket and began to drag him slowly across the floor toward the waiting elevator. His eyes were fixed on the little compartment, brightly lit and welcoming.

"Jans! It's Marz! I'm a mile out . . ."

Ardo glanced through the broken panes of the command deck. In the distance, to the west, he could just make out the Dropship: a dot silhouetted against the multiple contrails of Confederacy transport ships reaching into the sunset beyond.

"Don't you . . . orry broth . . . be . . . ith you . . . ust a few . . ."

Something bright fell between him and the elevator, splashing against the floor plate.

It was smoking where it landed.

Ardo quickly looked up.

A ribbon of molten silver ran in a ragged arc across the ceiling. Its curve continued toward itself, circumscribing a circle in the ceiling directly above the command island.

"Lieutenant! Move! Now!" Ardo screamed into the com channel.

Breanne and Littlefield looked up at the same time. The structural cross supports were melting under the rain of acid. Already they could hear the low groan of the metal giving way under its own weight.

They needed no further urging. Breanne leaped over the console bordering one side of the island. Littlefield grabbed Merdith's arm and ran for the stairs. He propelled her ahead of him, launching Merdith toward the catwalk around the room's perimeter before jumping clear himself.

With a wrenching groan, the ceiling of the Operations Room gave way, crashing downward toward the command island. The weight of the ceiling hull plates and cut structural supports crushed the island consoles with a thunderous sound. The entire communications antenna farm came crashing down with it, twisting into a barely recognizable tangle as the heavy hull plating slid down off the wrecked island and against the acid-weakened floor plates.

Ardo pulled furiously on Jans, trying to stay out of the way of the massive avalanche of writhing metal. The technician, however, was beginning to struggle against him as he regained consciousness. *His timing is lousy*, Ardo thought, but he needed this man to make his escape from this hell.

"Get ready!" Breanne shouted. "They're here!"

Breanne had already rolled painfully to her feet. A deep gash on her shoulder was bleeding freely through a tear in her combat suit. Littlefield was on the other side of the ruined island with Merdith. Ardo could see the two of them moving, trying to get around the wreckage to the elevator.

It was then that he spotted them: winged shapes rushing down through the ragged opening in the ceiling. The Mutalisks had carved a new way into the Command Center, scattering the humans from their protective cover. The prey were in the open now and vulnerable.

Ardo released Jans quickly beside him. They were at the open elevator. The now listless body lay across the threshold so as to keep the elevator door from closing again. It was all that the Marine had time to do before raising his weapon.

Merdith struggled to her feet, glanced up and screamed—more out of honest surprise than fear,

Ardo supposed. It was hard to think of that woman being truly afraid of much of anything. Whatever the reason, Ardo noted it got their attention. The remaining Mutalisks dove down through the opening, sailing into the room en masse.

Breanne did not wait. Her assault rifle began chattering away at once, slamming the winged nightmares into the wreckage. Two of them had impaled their wings on the twisted spikes of the broken antennae and support frames. They writhed and screamed in outrage against the indignity of being knocked out of the air, tearing themselves against the sharp edges of the torn metal.

Ardo had no time to concern himself with Breanne's fight, however. A leathery darkness of his own rushed toward him with impossible speed. He opened up with his own weapon, knocking it, too, out of the air. The creature refused to stop, however, and began writhing its way across the ruined floor. Ardo shredded its wings, blasting away at the membrane with deliberate effort. Some cool part of his mind took over, a part that he thought he would like to forget but that stepped forward now to save him when he needed it. Ardo ran as he fired, out of the alcove and toward his target. It continued to press toward him, relentless and heedless of the damage it was taking. Ardo continued to eat away at the creature's wings. *A few more feet should do it*, he thought. Ardo stepped slightly to his left.

The Mutalisk suddenly coiled, then sprang.

Ardo was waiting. He shifted his fire the moment the Mutalisk attacked. The stream of slugs from his rifle slammed against the chest bone of the Mutalisk, pushing it backward in midair and over the gaping chasm its brother had burned through the floor before him.

The Mutalisk flapped its wings but there was little left of them to catch the wind. It screamed in outrage as it tumbled down through the hole. Ardo stepped forward, shifting the stream of his fire now to the head as well as the chest and felt strangely satisfied.

"Thou shalt not kill . . ."

"An eye for an eye . . ."

"Love those that hate you . . ."

A wave of nausea passed over him, but he could not stop—would not stop. He shifted fire once more toward the Mutalisks still struggling to reach Breanne. Their combined fire was quickly shredding the beasts. Caught in the metal framework of the antennae, their own acid blood was working against them. Every wound ate into the metal around them, melting it and causing the antennae to collapse down on them even further, pinning them in place.

"Run! Merdith, run now!"

Ardo turned quickly toward the sound. It was Littlefield.

The sergeant was blasting away at a Mutalisk of his own, but it was dangerously close. Ardo could see from where he stood that the shower of acid from the approaching creature was eating into Littlefield's armor.

Merdith was behind him. They were both on the opposite side of the Command Center.

Littlefield's own stream of fire was ripping through the beast, showering the debris between them with smoking bits of ichor.

Merdith started to run, but the Mutalisk shifted toward her. Littlefield quickly darted between them, continuing his fire. The beast slithered toward them.

Ardo shifted fire from his own dying targets, but hesitated in frustration. The Mutalisk was between him and Littlefield. If he began firing on it, he would risk not only hitting both Merdith and Littlefield but spraying them with acid from the disintegrating creature. He yelled, "Littlefield! Get out of the way!"

Ardo could see the sweat beading on Littlefield's forehead.

The sergeant glanced at him, grinned, and then leaped directly toward the Mutalisk. Burying his weapon in the gut of the creature, Littlefield reached out with his free hand and gripped the monster by the throat. Enraged, the Mutalisk coiled its razor-edged tail around Littlefield.

"No!" Breanne roared.

"Run!" Littlefield shouted, his voice rising in agony. "Run, Merdith!"

The Mutalisk was coming apart under Littlefield's fire. The acid pouring from its body was melting the sergeant's combat suit, merging the two bodies hideously.

Merdith, the color drained from her face, ran

around the wreckage in the center of the room. She joined Ardo on the far side but could not bring herself to look.

Breanne moved up, shouting, screaming. "Get away, Littlefield! Let go and get away!"

Littlefield's weapon continued to fire. Ardo thought surely the flesh from his hand had been eaten away by now. Perhaps only the melting armor of the suit kept the gun firing. The Mutalisk stopped struggling as the pool of acid formed beneath them.

The floor plates groaned once more, and Sergeant Littlefield with his defeated foe vanished from view.

Ardo was shaking so hard that he found it difficult to hold on to his weapon. Outside they could hear a different scream, more familiar and higher pitched.

Merdith looked up toward the sound and then shouted, "Look!"

The Dropship. The *Valkyrie Vixen* hovered thirty feet away, its engines shrill and beautiful to their ears.

Ardo sucked in a ragged breath and turned around. Jans was leaning up against the side of the elevator, dazed but with his eyes open. Ardo stepped gingerly over to him across the buckled floor plates and pulled him to his feet. "Mister, it's time you got us the hell out of here."

They moved quickly toward the remains of the window. Ardo could see Marz through the cockpit canopy.

Breanne breathed out and then spoke. "We're leaving."

Merdith, standing beside her, seemed troubled. "Lieutenant, how many of those winged horrors did your sentries report inbound when all of this started?"

"Eight. Why?"

"Well, did any of your sentries report any kills? I mean, I don't think I . . ."

Breanne's eyes went wide. She turned to the Dropship and began waving at him. She was shouting. "Get out! Go around!"

He was smiling and waving back.

"No! Damn it! Get out!" Breanne shouted, waving more emphatically. "What the hell is the tactical channel? I can't seem to raise him on the—"

"Oh, no!" Merdith breathed.

The remaining three Mutalisks soared up over the command center. Marz was too intent on finding his brother to notice. By the time he realized they were on him, the Mutalisks were already disgorging their spawn into the engine intakes and against the canopy.

Breanne raised her weapon and began firing. Ardo joined her, but it was too little and too late. Desperately, Marz throttled open the engines and the unsuspecting Mutalisks were sucked into the intakes. The acid flowed into the engines, separating turbine blades from high-speed shafts. In moments the Dropship began tearing itself apart.

Marz managed to get his *Vixen* only a hundred yards to the west before it exploded, sending shards raining down throughout Scenic Outpost. It crashed into the ravine just west of the base, burning furiously as the hypergolic tanks collapsed.

Beyond the thick column of smoke, Ardo saw more Confederacy transports arch gracefully into the sky, their contrails glowing salmon-orange against the crimson horizon of the setting sun.

There were not nearly as many as he had seen before.

CHAPTER 19

DEBTS

ARDO STOOD IN SHOCK. HIS MIND DID NOT WANT to register what he had just seen. Suddenly, it seemed hard to breathe. He began gulping down long, shuddering breaths. What was there left to do?

He turned to face Lieutenant Breanne. Her eyes were staring unfocused at the burning hulk beyond the perimeter as though she were seeing completely through it.

"Lieutenant?" Ardo spoke quietly, somehow afraid to disturb her. "What do we do now?"

Breanne blinked. She did not—could not—look in his direction. "We . . . I . . . I don't . . . know. I . . ."

"What do I do, Lieutenant?" Ardo repeated, his voice shaking with an anger that was welling up from deep within him. "Give me an *order*, Lieutenant! Tell me what to *do*, Lieutenant! How do I *fix this for you, Lieutenant!*"

Breanne turned toward Ardo. Her eyes were

watery and unfocused. "I think . . . maybe Littlefield would . . ."

"Littlefield is *dead*, Lieutenant!" Ardo's voice was loud and shaking. The beast that always seemed caged somewhere in the back of his mind broke free, yelling into the face of his superior officer. "He's *gone!* He can't help you out of this one, Lieutenant! He's not going to save you. He's not going to make you look good. And he most definitely isn't going to keep you alive this time! It's *you*, Lieutenant, here and now! You give the orders! You show us the way out of—"

"Bernelli to command."

The tactical channel was still functioning. Bernelli's voice cut through some intermittent static.

Ardo stared at Lieutenant Breanne, waiting.

Breanne swallowed, beads of sweat forming on her forehead and among the bristle of her short-cropped hair.

"Bernelli to command; Come in, command."

Ardo grimaced and keyed the channel open on his own suit. "Bernelli," he replied curtly. "The lieutenant specifically ordered everyone to stay off this channel."

"Not much need, now, Ardo. They're leaving."

"What?"

"The Zerg. They're moving on past us to the west. The whole line of them just passed us right up."

"That doesn't make sense," Ardo mused over the channel.

"Sense or not, that's what they're doing."

"He's right, Melnikov." It was Mellish's voice this

time. *"I'm watchin' 'em through the bunker. They went by us like a line of locusts and left us behind. I've got a good eye on 'em through these field glasses and they're all slitherin' off to the west. I guess they're all lookin' forward to a night on the town."*

Ardo blew softly through his lips. Mar Sara City was to the west, now abandoned by the Marines and essentially defenseless.

"Cutter, this is Melnikov. I'm with the lieutenant in Operations—or what's left of it. Where are you?"

"I'm in Bunker Four on the southwest perimeter. What the hell happened up there? Where's Littlefield and the lieutenant?"

"Get up here on the quick," Ardo snapped without explanation. "The, uh, lieutenant needs you."

"Yeah, well, if the lieutenant needs me, she can ask for me, and not some snotty-nosed, trigger-happy preemie of a—"

"Cut the crap, Cutter," Ardo barked. "Lieutenant wants you here, so *move!*"

"On my way," Cutter responded in a cold tone. *"If nothing else, I'd be interested in seeing you. I hope you've kept that woman warm for me, preemie. I'm sure she'll be glad to see a man after having to put up with you."*

Ardo angrily keyed his tactical communications to Off, then turned toward the elevator bay. "I'm sorry, Merdith. I'll see to it that Cutter doesn't bother—"

The elevator door was closed. The indicator lights on the panel in the alcove showed the lift descending. A feeling of dread rushed over Ardo.

Merdith was gone.

Ardo cast his eyes quickly around the room. The fallen section of the overhead hull now sat at an awkward angle to the floor. The consoles on the left side of the command island were crushed nearly to the floor plates by its weight, but the right side remained elevated. Ardo quickly made his way across the buckled and acid-torn floor plates.

"Melnikov?" Breanne spoke as though she were just waking up. "Damn it! What the hell are you doing?"

"It was sitting on the floor just a few feet from me," Ardo muttered as he leaned forward peering between the consoles on the right side.

The box was gone, too.

Ardo roared, his voice a wordless expression of animal outrage. He glanced at the elevator. Too long, he realized. He'd never catch her that way. He turned and pulled himself up the short ladder to the catwalk that now was a ripple of bent metal around the room. Grasping the open pane of one of the shattered windows, he pulled himself forward into the howling wind and looked down.

The dark, curving hull dropped away below him in the fading twilight. Pools of light emanated dimly from the windows of the Command Center and from the anticollision markers that blinked mournfully from the various equipment pods jutting from the main hull. Just beyond the curve of the hull, a large bright patch of yellow light extended from the main doors of the Command Center across the small patch of compressed dirt between the dark patchwork of the base buildings.

There, a long shadow emerged. It was cast by a single, small female figure struggling to run with a heavy case.

Ardo glanced at the power indicators just below the lip of his helmet. He had not yet dipped into the power reserve. It would be plenty to catch up with her.

In a single movement, Ardo pulled himself through the window opening and began running down the slope of the Command Center. His booted footfalls rang against the hull as he made his way down the various sensor armatures around the hull. Such a suicidal dash would have been impossible without the combat suit, but despite the whine of the servos in complaint of the abuse, he quickly made his way down the ever-increasing slope of the outer hull. Merdith was running west toward the factory unit. Ardo checked her position as he ran. Within moments the slope became too steep to support him, but he was already within twenty feet of the ground. He held on to a protruding thruster pod for a moment, then jumped into the air.

He landed hard, rolling on the ground as his training had taught him. The suit absorbed most of the impact, the servos whining as he rolled to his feet and set off in pursuit at a dead run.

Turning the corner, Ardo saw an array of vehicles in front of him. Each had been parked outside of the automated factory that had churned them out on demand, only to be abandoned. The evening wind was whipping blinding dust between the various SCVs, ground support trucks, and a line of enclosed Vulture cycles.

Ardo stopped. She was in there somewhere, he knew. All he had to do was find her.

The wind was howling around his head, but he turned up the external audio sensors anyway. He switched the tactical channel to Standby. He knew Breanne would start asking after him soon enough, and he did not want the distraction.

Ardo moved slowly forward through the machines, stepping carefully and quietly. He thought absently how amazing it was that as complicated a piece of military hardware as a battlesuit was, it could still move with deadly quiet when required. He raised and readied his weapon. He knew that he was perfectly willing and able to shoot Merdith through the head if necessary—and quite possibly even if it was *not* necessary.

The sand-obscured SCVs stood as still as sentinels. The armored titans were just over ten feet tall. Ardo wove his way between them smoothly, his rifle at the ready.

Something creaked in the wind to his right. He spun around, his rifle quickly leveled in the direction of the sound. The vision augmentation in his closed faceplate illuminated the culprit at once: an open maintenance hatch on an SCV leg flapped in the wind. He turned back again on his ragged course, picking his way forward.

An engine turned over with agonizing slowness somewhere just ahead of him. Ardo smiled thinly to himself and stepped smoothly around another SCV that was blocking his line of sight.

It was a hauler, a truck nearly as tall as an SCV. The chassis was suspended between six massive balloon tires, three on a side. The control cab jutted out from the front. Ardo could just make out the glow from the cab's windows through the wind-whipped sand.

Getting into the cab was something of a problem. One had to climb up a vertical ladder to get to one of the side hatches. He could do it in the combat suit, of course, but he suspected the lieutenant would prefer Merdith alive. A direct assault was not the best way to achieve this objective. He suddenly had a better idea. Smiling to himself, he made his way around to the back of the vehicle, being careful to stay out of the sight lines from the extended mirrors on either side of the control cab. Then he ducked down and began crawling down the length of the truck chassis. Halfway down, he heard the low agony of the starter motor once again. He began to hurry. The engine sputtered twice, then died.

Under the cab, Ardo slowly brought himself into a crouch just below the driver's-side door. He could see shadows moving in the cab, heard various switches being toggled and Merdith's low mutters.

Ardo quickly stood up and wrenched open the

driver's-side door. With his free hand he grabbed the astonished Merdith by the arm, intent on pulling her out of the cab and throwing her to the ground.

Ardo jerked Merdith from the driver's seat in a single motion, his combat suit bringing him incredible strength. The woman tumbled out of the cab, her hands desperately fastening on Ardo's grip. Her flailing legs kicked against the truck cab, pushing Ardo unexpectedly backward with additional momentum. Ardo fell away from the cab, dragging the panicked Merdith with him.

Both of them tumbled to the ground. Ardo quickly rolled to his feet, his weapon already in hand by the time he was standing. Merdith lay painfully on the ground, groaning in the wind at his feet.

"Get up," he said. "You're going back."

Merdith looked up, gasping for air.

"You're my prisoner," he said flatly, raising his weapon.

"Prisoner?" she coughed, her words derisive. "Prisoner of *what*?"

"Prisoner of the Confederacy," Ardo explained dutifully.

Merdith snorted derisively. "That makes two of us."

"Shut up!" Ardo growled.

"Listen, I've been monitoring the com traffic from here." Merdith pointed up to the cab of the truck. "The Confederacy forces are done with their evac, soldier-boy. Hell, they're probably already out of the system by now."

"So we'll find another uplink!" Ardo was beginning to sweat. "We'll call for an evac. They'll come back and—"

Merdith snapped. "Wake up, Ardo! We're *supposed* to be *dead*! You think that nuke just dropped out of the sky on its own? We were all supposed to *eat* that nuke, soldier-boy! CHQ sent you and your pals out there to find me and my box—that goddamn poison box—and the moment they knew you had it they *called off* your evac and lobbed a big one with you and me and that box as ground zero. They knew your situation top to bottom. They set you up. The only reason they sent you out there was to find me and that lousy box and *die with it!*"

"We're soldiers, lady." Ardo's face flushed red. "Soldiers die! It's our *job* to die!"

"No." Merdith's voice lowered but remained intense. "It is your job to *fight*. You fought today and we lived. CHQ cut you off without a prayer and you *still* fought and you *still* lived. Make no mistake about it, Ardo. As far as they are concerned we are all dead and they prefer it that way. Jeez, they *planned it* that way! No one is supposed to know about this box. If you show up with it at CHQ, they'll make sure that you're all a whole lot deader than they *think* you are now."

"Shut up! Why the hell can't you just *shut up?*"

She pleaded with him over the screaming wind. "Don't throw away your life on phantoms, soldier-boy! The Confederacy lied to you, robbed you of your love, your family, and your entire past. They sent you here to do a dirty job for them, and once you did it they casually tried to murder you. Underneath all that programming and brainwashing and 'social reconditioning' there is still a man—Ardo Melnikov—who deserves to have a life and to live it." Merdith sighed into the wind. "There must be something left deep inside of that noble boy who was raised by loving parents."

Ardo blinked. He was sweating, and the combat suit cooling systems did not seem to be helping. "What . . . what are you suggesting? What are you saying?"

Merdith nodded, their eyes locked. "I'm saying we get out. They think we're dead—let's just leave it that way. We get off-planet and find a new life somewhere else and let someone else do the dying for us."

Ardo smiled sadly. "And just how are we supposed to leave? Walk? The Confederacy left. They took the last of the commercial transports with them. Even if I said yes, even if I trusted you, there's no way off this rock."

Merdith stepped forward, smiling. "Oh, yes, I think there is one way off this rock."

Ardo raised his gun slightly. Merdith took the hint and stepped back.

"The Sons of Korhal," she said levelly.

"The Sons of Korhal?" Ardo snorted. "A handful of delusional fanatics?"

"Yes." Merdith nodded, smiling. "Because a fleet of

transport ships of those 'delusional fanatics' is five hours out and inbound to this same rock right now. They'll be landing here to evac anyone they can—anyone who's left—and, my good soldier-boy, I suspect they will be especially anxious and grateful to accept our ticket."

Ardo shook his head but didn't say anything.

"Ardo, we give them that box and we're off on the first flight out!" Merdith pressed her point fervently. "All we have to do is get out of here with that box and stay alive for the next six hours. I know where there is an enclave, the last place the Zerg are going to move against. The Zerg will almost certainly move against the cities first."

"What?" Ardo suddenly realized what she was saying.

"The enclave should be able to hold out until the fleet arrives. The cities will slow the Zerg advance so we'll have enough time to—"

"The cities?" Ardo was suddenly galvanized by his own thoughts. "Civilians being slaughtered by those nightmares—thousands of them—and all you can do is count them by the number of minutes that they buy for *your* escape?"

Merdith swallowed hard. "We all have to make sacrifices, Ardo. Sometimes they're hard, but . . ."

Patriarch Gabittas was speaking to him in the seminary class. "What profit it a man if he gain the whole world and lose his soul . . ."

Melani smiled at him under a golden sun.

"And so their sacrifice—thousands of lives—has meaning because you and your precious rebellion can live?" Ardo shook with his anger. "Littlefield gave his life for you! He stepped up and threw his life down so that you could live. Isn't that enough? How many people is your life worth, Merdith? Hundreds? Thousands?"

Merdith's eyes flashed. Ardo turned angrily and raised his rifle overhead. With an outraged cry, he smashed the butt of the rifle through the lower window in the cab door. It didn't seem to help. He threw the weapon through the vacant pane into the cab with another howl. He turned back to Merdith, gripping her shoulders roughly with both hands.

"What about my life, Merdith? How many people is my life worth? How many should die for me?"

Ardo's grip tightened. Merdith winced in pain.

"What about my soul, Merdith? My soul is mine. No one can have it. Not the Confederacy. Not your precious rebellion. You can't buy my redemption. What is my life worth, Merdith? How many . . . how many people can I buy with my life?"

His father was reading to the family. "And fear not them which kill the body, but are not able to kill the soul: but rather fear him which is able to destroy both soul and body in hell.

Ardo stood frozen, transfixed.

Merdith looked up, still in his painful grip. "What is it?"

Melani stood in the field of golden wheat. She was handing him the box and reciting something from Scripture.

"Please." Merdith grimaced. "You're hurting me!"

"It is better that one man should perish than that a nation should dwindle and perish in unbelief . . ."

Ardo suddenly let Merdith go. "How many ships are coming?"

"What? Maybe a hundred—whatever they could scrape together, I guess—but they'll never reach the cities in time."

"No, but what if the Zerg didn't make it to the cities?" Ardo turned back to the truck as he spoke, pulling open the door and climbing up into the cab. "Thousands could be saved, couldn't they?"

"You can't stop the Zerg, soldier-boy!"

Ardo jumped back down from the cab.

In his hands he held the metal case.

"No, we can't," Ardo said. "But we might—just might—be able to slow them down."

CHAPTER 20

SIRENS

"YOU ARE COMPLETELY OUT OF YOUR FRAGGED mind, you know that?"

Ardo looked around the Operations Room. The faces he saw looking back at him for the most part seemed to be in agreement with Cutter's statement.

A cascade of sparks rained down from the ceiling of the Operations Room. Tinker was outside in an SCV. The technician had managed to clear most of the broken antennae and sensor probes away and lifted the fallen section of the hull back up to where it belonged. Now he was welding additional plating over the acid cuts in the metal overhead to hold it all in place and reinforce the structure.

The rest of the surviving detail had been called back into the Operations Room. Ardo was facing all that remained of the platoon that had left that same morning—a morning that seemed to Ardo to be years in the past. Private Mellish sat wearily on the catwalk, his legs dangling down over one of the console covers.

He was all that was left of Jensen's original squad and now apparently wanted to look anywhere but at Ardo. Privates Bernelli and Xiang stood leaning back against the floor consoles opposite Mellish. Xiang's eyes seemed unfocused and distant while Bernelli's appeared to bore right through Ardo with laser intensity. Lieutenant Breanne stood with her back turned to the room on the catwalk behind Xiang and Bernelli, her arms folded across her chest. One might have thought that she was gazing out the still broken window into the darkness beyond, but Ardo knew that she saw nothing out there and that her mind was very much in the room.

As was Cutter, the mammoth islander in the plasma Firebat suit, who was having no trouble expressing his views. He stomped back and forth across the newly welded floor plates in front of the elevator bay. "You are absolutely meltdown fragged in the head!"

"Maybe I am," Ardo said, fingering the metallic case resting awkwardly on the bent floor of the command island next to him. Merdith was leaning against the back of one of the crushed panels of the island, her hands in the pockets of her jumpsuit, her eyes cast down toward the floor in thought. "Maybe I am, but I don't see that it makes much difference to us, and it *might* make a lot of difference to someone else."

"Not much difference to us?" Cutter gaped. "You want to turn that Zerg homing beacon on—draw every Mutalisk, Hydralisk, and I-don't-know-what-lisk within a thousand clicks right down on top of us—and you figure we won't *care?*"

"That's not what I said." Ardo shook his head.

"By the gods, I hope *not!*"

"What I said was, it won't *make* much difference to us." Ardo set his combat helmet down on top of the case and removed his combat gloves. "Look, the Confederacy left us for dead—hell, they flat-out *wanted* us dead! They're not coming back for us even if they knew we were here. They've written off this entire world—and every colonist on it. Just think, Cutter! The Confederacy's little secret device here *called* the Zerg down on this world. We've got the proof right here in this box. You think they want any-body to know that they're responsible for the flat-out cue-balling of this entire planet?"

Bernelli spoke up. "But . . . but what about these Sons of Kohole or Korhal or whoever. They got evac ships coming. Can't we hook up with them?"

Ardo nodded. "We could barter with the Sons of Korhal. We could trade them this box and probably find a way off this planet, if anyone can. We'd have to break through the Zerg front, find them, and make the deal. But these Sons of Korhal have their own plan. The rescue ships they have coming certainly aren't enough to evac the entire planet. It's just public relations—show some pictures of them rescuing a few left behind. What they do *not* want everyone to know, however, is that they are also responsible for the Zerg coming here."

Xiang turned to Ardo suddenly. "The Korhal bunch? I thought that was a Confederacy gadget."

Ardo turned to Merdith. "Tell them."

Merdith squirmed uncomfortably. "It's true that you could make a deal with the Sons of Korhal—"

"No," Ardo said, and Merdith winced at his tone. "Tell them who activated the device!"

Merdith continued to look at the floor. "Some sacrifices have to be made for the continuation of the Cause. The . . . atrocities of the Confederacy leave the rebellion no choice . . . ah . . . but to use the device against further Confederacy aggression. By using their own weapon against them—"

"By the gods, Melnikov!" Xiang was shocked. "It's mass murder! Planetary genocide!"

Merdith looked up, her eyes flashing. "The Sons of Korhal have a legitimate claim to—"

Mellish spat on the floor in disgust. "Oh, shut up, lady! The Sons of Korhal don't give a shit about the civilians any more than the damn Confederacy does. Near as I can tell, they're just the flip side of the same coin—and just as tarnished."

Ardo shook his head sadly. "And when this is all over, this Korhal bunch certainly won't want us breathing any more than the Confederacy will. The Confederacy may have made the box, but it was the Sons of Korhal who opened it. We know what happened here and how many died . . . because of *both* sides." He sighed. "No, boys, we're all dead. About the only thing left for us to decide is *how* we die and what we die *for*."

"Well, isn't that a pretty speech," Cutter sniffed, his large nostrils flaring. "So you're all hero and sacrifice, are you, Melnikov? I've seen just how much of a hero you are, boy! You were perfectly willing to sacrifice Wabowski back there at Oasis—plenty willing, by my reckoning! Now you're all the big man wanting to sacrifice the rest of us!"

"There's families out there, Cutter." Bernelli sounded tired. "Women and children . . ."

"Yeah, and some of them are mine!" Cutter's deep black eyes were wide and watery. "But I didn't sign up for this!"

"Seems to me you wanted a fight when you landed on this rock," Mellish added, his words rising in tone. The private did not care for Cutter in the least. "Now you're looking for the back door?"

"Cutter never took a back door in his life, sister! Give me a stand-up fight! Bring 'em on and I'll eat their hearts for breakfast. But *this*,"—Cutter pointed angrily at Ardo—"*this* latrine cleaner tells me to sit still and *die* for a bunch of civvies I have never met, who will never know what I did for them and probably wouldn't give a shit even if they did! *That's* insane!"

"So that's why you're here, Cutter?" Ardo's frustration seeped into his voice. "You want someone to give you the credit? Throw you a parade or shed some tears? Is that what's important here, that you're remembered as the hero? Innocent people are gonna *die* out there, Cutter, and we're the only ones who can help them, whether they know it or not!"

"I'm here to find my brothers. They're out there and I've got to find them!"

Ardo was about to say something but stopped. Cutter's brothers. He had not thought about it much before now, but if his own memories had been so blatantly tampered with and altered by the resoc tanks, what had they done to the huge islander? Were his brothers even on this rock? Did Cutter, for that matter, in reality even *have* any brothers? How could Ardo possibly ever explain that to the volatile Marine?

Bernelli sighed. "Well, if we're gonna die, I'd like to at least know it was for something more than my pension."

"Well, if *I'm* going to die," Cutter seethed, "it won't be because of this butt wipe . . . and it won't be *alone!*"

Cutter moved so fast that Ardo had no time to react. In two quick steps the huge man crossed the floor and wrapped his right hand around Ardo's throat.

Ardo tried to speak, but he was not able. The Firebat suit reinforced Cutter's intense grip. Ardo struggled uselessly. In moments bright stars began to burst in his vision and the world began to blur. Everyone was shouting at once. Shadows moved around the periphery of his vision, but all he could see was the outraged face of the islander with murder in his eyes.

A voice. "Drop him! Drop him, now, Cutter!"

Suddenly, Cutter released him. Ardo tumbled like a cloth doll to the floor, gasping for breath. He looked up.

Lieutenant Breanne was holding her gauss rifle against Cutter's temple. "Cutter, you want to save your brothers? You ever think that they might be part of those civilians waiting for a way out of this? You ever think that the only way you're gonna have a chance of saving any of your brothers is by making sure those Zerg don't reach the city before the transports?"

Cutter blinked furiously. His voice was low and quiet when he replied. "No, ma'am. I . . . I hadn't thought of that."

"Then stop trying to think," Breanne screamed. Her voice was shrill and unnerving. "I'll think for you. You're not *paid* to think!"

Breanne pulled the weapon back from Cutter's head and motioned him back with its muzzle. "I've spent a lifetime fighting everyone else's wars, for other people's ideals and other people's causes! Melnikov is right! Each of our lives could buy hundreds of others, maybe thousands. They'll never know it, never appreciate it, but if I have to die, let me die for something worthwhile!"

Breanne turned to the box and with quick, firm

motions, released the latches. The metallic box was open.

The lieutenant turned to the astonished faces in the room. "We have, by my rough estimate, approximately an hour and a half before the first Zerg arrive. I suggest that we make use of the time."

Ardo was on his fourth trip to the various bunkers. He was tired, but he knew that he would not have to be tired much longer. There was a peace waiting for him that was long and permanent. He found that he was rather looking forward to it. The teachings of his youth kept bubbling back to the surface of his memory: tales of faith and hope and peace in an afterlife. Strange, he thought, to consider such things here in the center of hell.

Tinker had been using the SCVs to construct several new bunkers around the Command Center. This would be the defensive core inside the outer perimeter. They would start their defense on the outer ring, taking ranged shots on the approaches to the base. When the Zerg threatened to overrun the outer position, then the plan was to fall back to the inner ring of linked bunkers for the final defense. After that, they would hold on as long as they could . . . and hope that it was long enough.

Meanwhile, Mellish had taken a couple of the others out in an APC with every mine they could salvage from the compound. Ardo had grinned when Mellish had come to him with the idea. Now the private was out happily sowing mines in a specific pattern around the compound as though he were a farmer working the back forty. Ardo hoped Mellish would enjoy a bumper crop from the seeds he was sowing.

Ardo busied himself in the factory manufacturing new ammunition for the rifles. Breanne had even taken Ardo's point about the Zerg never stopping for their wounded. It was a fairly easy calibration. Rather than the standard infantry rounds, he reprogrammed the replicator to produce hollow-point spread rounds. Unlike their standard issue, these rounds would flatten and expand on impact with the target. These were not designed to wound, but to kill and inflict as much damage as possible. Ardo was looking forward to seeing if they worked.

Tinker was still working on the south perimeter bunker as Ardo approached. Tinker had not said more than ten words to anyone since his brother's Dropship went down. Ardo was more than a little concerned about the man, but there was no time to deal with his problems at the moment—perhaps no time to deal with them ever. Ardo walked up to the low domed building and entered the open access hatch.

Bunkers were standard equipment for SCV manufacture, and it could truly be said that once you had seen one bunker, you had seen them all. Their thick metal shell held sufficient quarters for four, with weapons ports on all sides. They were not the most comfortable of quarters, but they had the benefit of being as safe a place as you could find on any

Confederacy base. Once assembled, they were incredibly difficult to take apart. Just how difficult he was sure they were about to learn.

He stepped into the central compartment, loaded down with his ammo cases, and was surprised to see Merdith staring out of one of the weapons ports.

"Oh, excuse me," Merdith said. "I'll get out of your way."

"No, it's all right." Ardo set the boxes down and began stowing them under each of the weapons ports. "You're no trouble. If you're here for the view, you're looking in the wrong direction."

"Yeah. I never was one for being a tourist." Merdith laughed tiredly. Then she turned back to the port. "Which way do you think they'll come first?"

"I don't know," Ardo said, moving to stand next to her and gazing out across the red plain. "The last units we saw were passing to the west. My guess it that they will be the first to arrive. I'd look for unwanted company coming from there first."

Merdith nodded. A short silence passed between them.

"Hey, soldier-boy?"

"Yes, ma'am?"

"If I don't get a chance to tell you . . . I think what you've done here is . . ." Her voice trailed off.

Ardo glanced at her. "Is what?"

"I . . . I don't know. I was going to say 'good' or 'right' but the words didn't seem quite big enough." She rested her folded arms on the sill of the weapons port, laying her head down on them as she spoke. "Maybe even . . . epic."

Ardo laughed. "Epic?"

Merdith laughed, too. "Okay. Maybe not epic, either. Whatever it is, I'd like to tell you thanks."

"I wouldn't thank me, ma'am. I just got us all killed."

"But how many more are going to live because of what we do here? I'd never really thought of it before." Merdith looked at him. "They may not say thank you. They may never know what happened here or even who we were, but I'll say thanks for them."

Ardo nodded, then thought for a moment. "You know . . . I'm not even sure of who I am anymore. I've been programmed and reprogrammed so many times that I've forgotten who I was and why I was and where I was even going. Yet there was always *me* here somewhere—that part of my soul that they could never program over or take away. I used to fear that, but now it's all I have to hang on to. You helped me find my soul, ma'am, and for that, *I* want to say thanks to you."

Ardo reached down picked up a new gauss rifle, and tossed it over to Merdith. He said, "You know how to use it, don't you?"

Merdith caught the rifle, then primed it expertly with a single motion. "You trust me with this?"

"Hey, if you kill one of *us*, it just means there's one less person to watch *your* back!" Ardo smiled.

Merdith smiled back. "I'll have to be careful about that, won't I?"

"I wish you had met Melani. I doubt you'd have had much in common, but she—"

"Mellish reporting. I've got a visual from the west. We've got company."

Ardo grimaced. "They're early."

CHAPTER 21

SEIGE

"*STAND BY, PEOPLE!*" IT WAS BREANNE'S VOICE over the tactical net. "*Outer perimeter first, then fall back on my command to the inner perimeter. Flash status!*"

Ardo keyed his tac-com transmit key twice. "Melnikov, Outer Five, southwest."

"*Mellish, Outer Four, northwest! They're comin' hard and—*"

"*Cut the chatter, Mellish! Flash status!*"

"*Xiang. I'm here. Outer Three, northeast.*

"*Bernelli at Outer Two. I'm . . . uh . . . I'm southeast.*

"*Cutter, Outer One, south, Lieutenant.*"

"*Status complete! Hold fire until they breach the outer mines. Report the breach, then open fire, understood?*"

Ardo smiled. Even in the middle of a hopeless cause, Breanne was going to do this by the numbers. If there was a way to *die* by the numbers, he knew that she would do it, too.

"What is it?" Merdith asked, seeing the look on Ardo's face.

He leaned forward, his eyes narrowing as he peered out the firing slits in the bunker.

"By the gods! What *is* that?" Merdith breathed in disbelief.

The horizon to the southwest was blurred, its crisp line smudged. It might have been a sandstorm rolling toward them, but Ardo knew it was something far more deadly.

Ardo opened the tac-com channel. "Lieutenant; Melnikov. I've got a line of Zerg approaching rapidly from the west . . . about three clicks out. I can't make out the ends of the line."

"Mellish here. I think I have the end of the line of advance here on about a two-ninety radial. Hell, I didn't think there were that many Zerg in the whole—"

"This is Cutter. I can't seem to make out the end of the line on my end."

"Ardo! What's going on?"

The Marine looked over at Merdith. "What? Oh, *damn!* You don't have a tactical com set. That's them coming now—a line of Zerg that just about covers the horizon and God only knows how deep they are behind that line. That little box of yours apparently works a lot better than I thought."

"So." Merdith swallowed hard, her mouth suddenly dry. Her fingers gripped her rifle so hard they were white. "What happens now?"

"We wait for them."

"Wait?" Merdith blinked. "Wait for what?"

"Wait until they hit the mine perimeters." Ardo

shook his shoulders and rolled his head. He was tense, and that was a bad way to go into battle. "Mellish and Bernelli sowed two perimeters of minefield around the base. There's one at a thousand meters and a second at five hundred meters. They're a combination of hopper and shape-charge mines with heuristic sensor links—"

"Whoa, slower! They've got heuristic what?"

"Sensor links. The mines talk to each other on a dedicated, low-power network and learn from each other what to look for in an enemy passing over them. The more they detonate, the smarter they get about killing whatever crosses them. Then they can modify their own blast patterns to maim more effectively. We've had to change their programming a little . . ."

"Because you don't want them just to maim," Merdith finished for him. She turned to gaze out the gun port of the bunker. The hazy line was getting much closer. "You want them to kill as many and as quickly as possible."

"That's right," Ardo replied, then leaned even closer to the gun port. "Incredible! Just listen to that."

The low rumble was felt before it could be heard— a pounding of the ground that nervously shook everything resting on top of it. In moments it grew to audibility—thousands of Zerg rushing heedlessly toward them in an enraged fury. The ear-piercing screech of their voices punctuated the roar, chilling Ardo to his bones.

"By the gods! What have we done?" Bernelli yelled across the com channel.

"Hold your fire!" Breanne's voice crackled over the channel in response. *"I've got to know where they hit the perimeter first!"*

A single dull thud shook the bunker. Dust from the upper ammunition racks sifted loose toward the floor. Ardo saw Merdith's eyes go wide. Then a quick succession of thuds rolled through the open ports.

"Bernelli here! Perimeter contact at radial two-twenty!"

The mine explosions rattled in quick succession now, one nearly on top of the other. They were sounding closer to Ardo.

"They're shifting!" Bernelli shouted. *"They're coming left, Melnikov!"*

Ardo quickly picked up his field glasses. He pushed Merdith back and pressed the glasses through the rightmost gun port.

He could see them clearly now: a solid wall of Zerg writhing and squealing nearly a thousand meters away. Every kind of hideous nightmare of their kind seemed to be present, charging in his direction, and then, as though heeding some unheard dance music, they all began shifting to the right.

The thudding explosions followed them. A wall of dirt, flame, and torn flesh surged into the air like a continuous curtain of death. Each Zerg in its turn charged forward, probing for the weak spot in the perimeter, searching for the opening that humans always left in the field through which they could pass and attack. Ardo smiled. He was looking into the mind of his enemy and knew something it did not know: that there was no opening through which they could pass because they knew they would never be leaving.

"Melnikov here!" Ardo shouted into the com channel over the thunderous barrage. "They're throwing their lead elements against the perimeter. Moving eastward around the outer minefield. Cutter? You got 'em?"

"Yeah, I see. Sweet Sister Sin! Look at 'em! They're moving to surround the base! I've never seen so many ugly bastards in my life! Come to me, you sweet meat! I'm digging a pit just for you! I'll roast you for dinner, you ugly—Heads up! Incoming!"

The curtain of destruction continued to explode before him, cutting off all sight of the Zerg beyond it. Ardo frantically searched with his field glasses for some sign of a breakthrough.

"The towers have a lock! Weapons release!"

He heard it before he saw it. The rockets leaped from the defensive towers. Merdith's scream was obliterated by the wail of the high-speed thrusters clawing their way toward the Zerg. Ardo followed their trails to their targets: Mutalisks in droves were soaring over the mine perimeter, their numbers nearly blanking out the bright sky beyond. The rockets slammed into them, their bright blossoms burning into the creatures with deadly accuracy. The beasts began falling like a grotesque rain on the perimeter area. A few of them triggered mines of their own when they slammed into the ground, but Ardo noted with grim satisfaction that the mines were already recognizing these new targets as being dead when they landed and were saving themselves for better and more threatening targets.

Suddenly, an almost deafening silence descended. The smoke and dirt around the perimeter began to settle, its curtain falling slowly back to earth.

Merdith and Ardo glanced at each other. The quiet after the initial barrage was unnerving.

"It stopped them." Merdith smiled, almost giddy at the thought. "Ardo! It's incredible! You stopped them!"

Ardo lifted his glasses once more and tried to peer beyond the settling dust, smoke, and debris. He could see them moving, shifting positions.

"Oh, damn," Ardo's voice shuddered as he spoke. "They've figured it out."

Merdith looked desperately out of the gun port, trying to see what Ardo was seeing. "Figured it out?"

Ardo keyed open his com. "Melnikov here! They're spacing out! Get ready for it!" Then he turned to Merdith. "Arm your weapon! This is it! The Zerg are spacing themselves out so that the mines will only take out one of them at a time. Then they'll charge the minefield all the way around."

Merdith's jaw dropped. "You mean . . . That's suicide!"

"No," Ardo said, quickly priming his own gauss rifle and laying its muzzle through the gun port. "That's just the Zerg. They don't value individual lives. That's why they don't bother with the wounded. They're cold and they're cunning, and they'll do whatever it takes to get to us and that box. They'll throw thousands of their warriors at us and won't think a second thought. They know that they won't run out of Zerg before we run out of mines."

"They're bringing up the Zerglings!" It was Cutter's voice. *"Guess they're wanting to keep the big boys for after they've cleared the minefield."*

"Setting the mines to discriminate. We'll let the smaller ones through both perimeters for now and concentrate the mines on the larger targets."

"Roger, Lieutenant. Here, kitty, kitty, kitty . . ."

Even with his unaided eyes, Ardo could see the changes in the Zergs a thousand meters out. The larval Zerglings were the smallest creatures known among the Zerg, the closest thing the monsters had to children. Ardo thought bleakly that it was another clear difference between their races, but then wondered if it was such a difference after all. Humans seemed equally willing to throw their own youth away on war, and Ardo knew that he was ample evidence of that.

"Here they come!" Bernelli announced, his voice rising. *"Make 'em count!"*

The multilegged Zerglings began skittering across the blackened and pocked ground of the outer perimeter. Ardo snapped shut his combat helmet, saw the targeting display come up at once, and began aiming his gauss rifle at the nearest of the creatures.

The targeting was eerily effective. The laser designator pinpointed the location of Ardo's shots. The gun jerked repeatedly with each shot as he shifted targets quickly from one Zergling to the next. The new ammunition was doing its job well. The explosive-tipped bullets smashed open the carapace of each approaching Zergling, blowing open the exit wound in a horrific, deadly display.

"Whoo-ho! It's a shootin' gallery out here!"

"I'm goin' for the high score today, Marines!"

How does this game end? Ardo thought. He continued to shift targets, but he was firing faster and faster trying to keep up with the onslaught. It was like trying to push back the tide. The Zerglings continued to come in wave after wave . . . and they were nearing the inner minefield.

Ardo glanced at Merdith. Her weapon had a built-in target designator. Her grip on the weapon had not eased as she fired faster and faster.

Suddenly, a deafening, high-pitched shriek from a thousand Zerg tore across the sand.

Shaken, Ardo's eyes went wide. "They're charging!"

The second line of Hydralisks thundered toward the outer minefield. Instantly the entire perimeter exploded in a deafening cacophony of fury and death. The defensive towers erupted again as well, the Mutalisks driving forward at the same time. Again the Mutalisk dead rained down, but their bodies were falling closer and closer to the outer walls of the base. Ardo could not be distracted, however. The crawling carpet of Zerglings was crossing the inner minefield and was now only five hundred meters away and closing quickly on the outer wall.

Ardo's gun suddenly went dry. He ejected the clip and slammed home another from the racks above him. When he raised his weapon again, the Zerglings were within four hundred meters.

"Lieutenant! The Zerglings are about to pass the inner mines!" Ardo called out over his quick succession of shots. "We're not holding 'em!"

"You've got to hold! We need the mines for the bigger Zerg!"

The Zerglings were within a hundred meters. Closing in on the base, they were forced by their numbers to come closer together, a nearly solid carpet of scarablike locusts looking, in Ardo's mind, to devour Ardo personally. Ardo switched his rifle to automatic and began spraying the approaching horde indiscriminately.

He was so preoccupied that he failed to register the thunderous sound of the mine detonations suddenly dropping off in the distance beyond. It shocked him when in a flash they resumed, this time only five hundred meters out. Towering columns of smoke, dirt, and rock shredded the charging Zerg. Their deafening roar surrounded the entire base as they charged from all sides simultaneously. The sun was blotted out by the waves of destruction. The detonations, no longer distinguishable one from another, now merged into one seemingly continuous demonic roar.

Stones and charred Zerg flesh began raining down on the bunker and the space beyond. Ardo continued playing his deadly stream of explosive shells against the Zerglings, who were now within a few meters of the bunker. Beyond them, the demon wall of death continued to march toward him, its sound shaking the plates of the bunker and threatening to knock him off his feet. The wall of mine explosions was now within a hundred meters of his position.

Ardo knew that the minefield ended within eighty meters of where he stood.

"Lieutenant! They're breaking through!"

"Fall back! Fall back now!"

Ardo did not have to hear the order twice. He grabbed Merdith's arm, quickly pulling her away from the gun port. He shouted. "We gotta go *now!*"

Merdith stepped quickly back from the port. As she did, the armor plates above the port began to peel upward.

A Zergling scrambled through the opening, hit the floor, and instantly leaped toward her.

Ardo fired his weapon, slamming the creature

away from her in midair, exploding it across the front wall of the bunker.

"Fall back!" Ardo yelled at her. "Run!"

The last thing Ardo saw as he slammed the hatch closed behind him was a wall of Zergling underbellies covering the gunports as they climbed up toward the torn opening.

CHAPTER 22

FAREWELL

THE SOUND WAS OVERWHELMING. THE DEFENsive towers were firing into the sky, disgorging their contents in a frenzy of flame and destruction. The missiles must have been arming just as they left their protective tubes, since their targets were close and pressing closer still.

Merdith ran in front of Ardo. The dusty stretch of ground between the outer wall and the inner bunkers was a veil of ash, smoke, and burning Zerg falling like a black snow from the sky. Acid splashes smoked against the ground here and there. Ardo followed the woman quickly. The intervening street between them and the inner bunker complex had never looked so far before.

Ardo sprang into the street at once. He looked up as he ran, desperate to protect himself. The defensive towers above him were scarred with repeated acid splashes, two of them already twisting under their own weight on their weakened frames. The sky beyond them was a roiling wall of flame and smoke with occasional patches of sky flashing through by some whim of chaos.

The bunker was ahead of him. Its main hatch stood open. Framed in it, he could see someone waving him onward.

Then he heard it—a sound he had heard before. It was a thunderous roar that overwhelmed even the sound of their own desperate battle. He looked up.

The rescue transports! They were coming in hot, bleeding off their speed in enormous heat through the atmosphere. The Sons of Korhal ships arched through the sky, their flaming contrails falling toward Mar Sara Starport to the west. They would be on the ground soon—their most vulnerable time as the ships tried to evacuate anyone who could reach them.

Time. They needed more time . . .

Gauss rifles suddenly chattered to life through the gun ports on either side of the bunker hatch, shocking Ardo into action. He leaped for the hatchway. Hands grabbed him and pulled him inside. His feet barely cleared the hatch seals before it slammed closed.

Ardo scrambled to his feet. Merdith was firing a stream through one of the gun ports. Bernelli had pulled him in, yelled something unintelligible at him, and then jammed his own rifle through the second set of gun ports.

Ardo quickly took his place beside Bernelli, positioned his gun, and then looked down his sights into hell.

Hydralisks were pouring over the base outer wall. They had thrown enough of their own against the minefield until there was nothing left to explode. There must have been thousands dead surrounding the complex but still they kept coming. Now they slid like a terrible wave over the wall, approaching the bunker en masse.

The tactical channel continued to chatter.

"Xiang! Report!"

"Xiang's down, Lieutenant! We've gotta get outta here! I can't hold 'em back!"

Bernelli continued to yell as he fired. Ardo joined him, the exhilaration of the sound in his own ears driving him as he poured death from the muzzle of his rifle.

Still the tide of dark horror tried to advance over the bodies of their own dead, but now the constricted field of fire was working against them, The dead were piling up before them, but they were not getting any closer to the bunker.

"Melnikov! You copy?"

Ardo ejected a cartridge, holding the fire trigger down even as he was slamming the new cartridge home. "A little busy here, Lieutenant!"

"We're coming in!"

"What?!"

"We're falling back to your position!"

"Affirmative," Ardo grimly replied. "Bernelli, keep 'em off! I'll get the back door!"

Ardo moved to the back section of the bunker. Through the ports he could barely see the vehicle pad off to his left. Behind that, he could make out the other two bunkers on either side of the Command Center. The left bunker had been Xiang's but was swarming with Hydralisks. Ardo could see them tearing at the plating, pulling apart the seams even as the bunker burned furiously. *Good-bye, Xiang,* Ardo thought.

Hydralisks were also tearing at the bunker on the right, but there a bright light suddenly flared to life. *Cutter,* Ardo realized. The rolling flames from the Firebat's plasma weapon were getting closer and closer. Ardo pressed his weapon through the port and blasted away at the Hydralisks trying to flank his own bunker and get to easier targets. At the last moment, Ardo smashed his hand against the release and opened the rear hatch.

Breanne stumbled through first, dragging the cursed box and Tinker Jans with it. They all fell heavily to the plated flooring. Cutter stood in the open hatchway, his plasma fire scorching several enraged Hydralisks in the process. With a final burst, Cutter took a step back through the hatchway. Ardo instantly slammed the hatch shut.

They were firing from all points around the bunker now. The dead Zerg were piling up in shining heaps.

Suddenly, the Zerg stopped advancing. The Hydralisks drew back into the shadows of the inner base complex. Within moments, there were no targets left to them, and their firing stopped.

"Hey, what's going on?" Cutter demanded. "They givin' up?"

Lieutenant Breanne was breathing heavily, whether from adrenaline or exertion, Ardo could not tell. "No. They *never* give up. They're just drawing up their forces . . . gathering strength. As soon as they're ready, they'll walk in here and take us."

Bernelli laughed nervously. "Oh, well, as long as we're not losing . . ."

"We *are* losing," Breanne said, flipping open her helmet and pushing her fingers back through her short-cropped hair. "We won't last ten minutes in here once they decide to make their move. You saw those ships coming down on Mar Sara! They're on the ground right now—fat civilian transports shoveling passengers in with a loader if they can. They're sitting ducks on the ground, and I can tell you that the best of them won't be able to get turned around inside forty minutes. Some longer."

"So?" Bernelli shrugged. "These Zerg slugs couldn't cross that distance in half a day, let alone an hour."

"The problem isn't the crawlers," Merdith shook her head. "It's the flyers—the Mutalisks. The only thing holding them here is that box. As soon as it's destroyed, the flyers will head straight for the starport, and all this would have been for nothing."

"All we need is to hold out for thirty minutes," Ardo said. "Just a lousy thirty minutes."

"Yeah," Breanne sneered. "And who's gonna buy you those thirty minutes?"

"I will."

They all turned.

It was Tinker Jans.

"I'll do it. I'll buy you your thirty minutes," the engineer said coolly. "But I'll need help."

Bernelli glanced out the port. "Hey, I think they're moving up!"

"You've got to get me into an SCV!" Jans said. "You've got to do it now!"

Breanne thought for a moment, then decided. "Cutter! Melnikov! You heard the man! Get him to an SCV!"

"There's definite movement out there!" Bernelli yelled.

Ardo punched the rear hatch release. Grim-faced, Cutter jumped out through the opening. Jans followed him, looking shaky and vulnerable in his soiled fatigues. Ardo ducked out after them, snapping closed his combat helmet—not that he thought it would help him much.

The ground was carpeted with the mutilated bodies of Zerg attackers. There was no time to think. They ran toward the vehicle pad, stumbling across the slick, greasy ground.

The nearest SCV stood silhouetted against the burning factory unit. Jans released the front access hatch, which popped open with a satisfying hydraulic whoosh.

"Come on! Come on!" Cutter encouraged nervously.

Jans clambered up the footholds in the face of the suit and settled backward into the control cabin. The access hatch started to lower smoothly.

"Here they come!" Breanne called out.

Ardo could see them. They were charging around the factory, over the compound wall, around the Command Center. They were everywhere.

"Now what do we do?" Cutter demanded of the engineer.

"Get back inside! Quickly!" Jans replied.

"And leave you here?" Ardo was shaken.

"Do it now, and just keep 'em off me as long as you can!"

Ardo had no time to argue. He and Cutter ran back toward the bunker. He could already see the tracer fire ripping through the gun ports in all directions. The Hydralisks were pouring across the ground, surging toward the bunker itself. Their carapace shells were distended, their armor-piercing spine quills at the ready for the attack.

Ardo fell back through the hatchway just as the Hydralisks attacked. The spines shot through the open hatch, slicing through the outer layers of his combat suit as though it were cotton cloth. Searing pain erupted in his leg, a quill having passed completely through and lodging in a neosteel beam.

Cutter helped him off the floor. "You dead yet?"

Ardo winced, unwilling to look at his leg. "Not yet."

They both took up their own port firing positions, dreading what was coming next.

The hull of the bunker suddenly rang with the sound of a thousand armor-piercing darts. It was a deadly hail, hammering repeatedly on the metal exterior, the acid-coated quills shearing away pieces of the metal shell with each impact.

"Kill them! Kill them all before they can get to us!" Breanne raged. The hull overhead was already buckling downward, large indentations pressing down into their space.

Firing desperately through the port, Ardo saw the SCV start to move.

The motion barely attracted the attention of the Zerg around them. The creatures appeared so intent on reaching the bunker that they barely took notice of the single craft.

If I could just get to one of those Vulture cycles, Ardo thought to himself wildly. *I could slip away . . . I could . . .*

He shook his head. Who would die because he lived? How *many* would die because he ran when his own life could buy so many others? No one would ever know who he was or why he was here. Anyone who ever cared for him would never know his fate. Maybe God would know. No matter what the Confederacy told him he was, Ardo knew who he was at last, and that he had something of his own that he could give.

The SCV lumbered up to the bunker complex. Tinker had left a stack of armor plating next to the bunker. Ardo wondered suddenly if the engineer had planned this all along. Jans picked up the plating with the massive arms of the SCV, looked at the bunker, found the weakest point, and slammed the plate across it. Holding it in place with one mechanical arm, Jans activated the plasma welder on the other and began reinforcing the hull.

The Zerg must have realized what Jans was doing. Several of the Hydralisks wheeled suddenly on the SCV.

Cutter and Ardo both saw it. In a moment, they shifted their fire. "Keep 'em off him, he said!" Cutter sneered through his sweat. "And just how are we supposed to do *that?*"

Jans continued to work frantically around the bunker, welding, reinforcing, replacing plates as quickly as possible. The Marines kept up their stream of death against the invaders, knocking down the Hydralisks in row after row as they advanced and fired.

The battle raged in an agonizing stalemate. Ardo's gun was hot in his armored hands. Somehow, Jans was keeping up with the repairs as quickly as the Hydralisks were damaging the bunker.

"Hey, I think it's working!" Bernelli laughed. "I think—"

The Hydralisks surged forward.

"No!" Ardo raged.

Jans could not see them coming in the SCV. Several of the Hydralisks had gotten shots at the work vehicle, and it was badly damaged but still operating. Suddenly, the fiendish wave had reached him. They were swarming about the SCV. Jans tried to beat them off the shell of the machine. In moments, however, they had dragged him and the entire SCV up and out of sight of the gun ports.

"They've got Jans!" Cutter yelled.

"We lose him and we're done for!" Breanne yelled back.

With a terrible cry, Cutter hit the hatch switch and dove outside.

Great sheets of plasma flame erupted outside the ports. Ardo could barely make out what was happening outside. Then he caught a glimpse of Cutter, his huge form standing outside the hatchway pouring out his superheated carnage.

Ardo's gun suddenly silenced. He ejected his cartridge instantly and then reached for the next in the overhead rack.

There was none.

"I'm out!" Ardo shouted.

Breanne tossed him another clip. "Make it count, kid. We're all low!"

He slammed home the clip and turned back toward the port.

Cutter was gone.

Ardo looked desperately through the ports but could not see the huge man anywhere. "Tinker!" he called through the tac-com channel. "Where's Cutter?"

"They . . . gone . . . they're all over me! Can't last . . ."

Breanne pitched back from the gun port. A single spine from a Hydralisk had found its way through the port opening, slamming through the faceplate of the lieutenant's combat suit. Hideously, it passed through her head and pinned her combat helmet to a neosteel support. Lieutenant L. Z. Breanne hung there, still standing.

Ardo glanced at Bernelli and then at Merdith. "I'm going out to save Jans. He can buy you some time. Bernelli, you got a clip left?"

"Yeah," he sighed.

Ardo looked at Merdith. "He'll take care of you."

Merdith nodded and looked away.

"See you on the other side," Ardo said to them both, then turned to the rear hatch.

"Hey, soldier-boy?"

He turned back to Merdith.

"Please, Ardo!" She wept. "Don't leave me alone!"

"Thanks, soldier-boy."

Ardo nodded, then hit the switch.

The gauss rifle responded instantly to his trained hand. The Confederacy had taught him well. His swiftly shifting aim kept the Hydralisks at bay and blew them clear of the SCV as well. As he stood there in the doomed yard, his sensations seemed heightened. The world around him was clearer than he had remembered it in years, perhaps clearer than he had ever experienced it. He took it all in: the horror around him that he was keeping at bay, the smoke over the compound that had turned to wisps in the lowering twilight. The sounds. The smells. All were alive for him.

Ardo was himself at last. He knew there was something that could never be taken from him: a victory more glorious and satisfying than anything experienced on any real field of battle.

As the last of his ammunition ran out, Ardo looked up. The transports, heavy with their precious human cargo, were arching into the sunset of his most glorious day. A hundred—maybe a thousand—cascades of thunderous exhaust climbed skyward. They would never know who had fought so hard for their lives. They would never hear his name nor sing songs to praise him. He alone would know of his triumph.

As the darkness closed over him, Ardo smiled at his last thought.

The contrails of the escaping ships . . . were all golden.

ABOUT THE AUTHOR

Tracy Hickman is a *New York Times* bestselling author best known for his *Dragonlance* series of novels co-authored with Margaret Weis. Born in Salt Lake City, Utah, in 1955, Tracy now lives and writes with his wife, Laura, in southern Utah.

Other novels in the worlds of
BLIZZARD ENTERTAINMENT

STARCRAFT #1: LIBERTY'S CRUSADE by Jeff Grubb
STARCRAFT #2: SHADOW OF THE XEL'NAGA
by Gabriel Mesta
DIABLO #1: LEGACY OF BLOOD
by Richard A. Knaak
DIABLO #2: THE BLACK ROAD by Mel Odom
WARCRAFT #1: DAY OF THE DRAGON
by Richard A. Knaak
WARCRAFT #2: LORD OF THE CLANS
by Christie Golden

And coming soon:

DIABLO #3: THE KINGDOM OF SHADOW
by Richard A. Knaak
WARCRAFT #3: THE LAST GUARDIAN by Jeff Grubb